THE BOUNDARY RIDERS

THE
BOUNDARY
RIDERS

JOAN PHIPSON

ILLUSTRATED BY MARGARET HORDER

HARCOURT, BRACE & WORLD, INC., NEW YORK

To Winifred West

CONTENTS

THE BOUNDARY RIDERS

ONE
PREPARATIONS

The Thompsons moved to Rosedale when Jane was thirteen and Bobby was eleven. Up till then their lives had been spent on the far western property that Mr. Thompson had inherited from his father. After that flat, dusty land with its wide horizons and difficult climate, they liked the cooler, more verdant hills and valleys of the middle west district around Rosedale. There were times when the children missed the big expanses and the old friends, for no one is ever entirely happy to leave his first home; and the fact that they were now within riding distance of a small country school was a black mark against Rosedale. But, as Mr. Thompson had explained, this was one of the reasons he had bought the property. The other was Mrs. Thompson's health, which had not proved equal to both heat and correspondence school on top of the ordinary domestic work. This reason Jane and Bobby found unanswerable.

Because Rosedale was so much smaller, it could not support the number of station hands that the old place had needed, and Mr. Thompson often found himself obliged to rely on the assistance of his children. Thus in a very short time, Rosedale became much more their own than the far western property ever had. As Australian properties go, it was smallish, but it was rich and well-situated on the northern edge of the high, rough country through which runs the Abercrombie River in central New South Wales. From the front veranda of the small brick homestead, it was possible to see the distant timber-covered hills rearing from mysterious blue depths and rising and falling against the horizon like some tumultu-ous and remote southern sea. Bobby had often looked at them and wished that their own boundary did not stop short of the first of the rugged foothills. No sign of life was ever visible on them, for they grew nothing that would attract sheep or cattle, and men wanting to make a living from the land gave them a wide berth. Perhaps it was because they were so unwelcoming that Bobby wanted to know them better. Or perhaps they offered him a challenge.

At eleven Bobby was thin, freckled, and silent, with pale blue eyes and bony knees that generally had scabs on them. He was not a boy that motherly ladies longed to cuddle, nor had he ever been. Even when his hair still bore traces of the infant gold and his face was still softly round and unfreckled, the glance from his blue eyes was remote and calculating, and his mouth was close and secret. He was accustomed to working out his own problems, and he kept his own counsel.

Jane, on the contrary, was exuberant, voluble, and enthusiastic about practically everything. She was reasonably tall for thirteen and inclined to be stocky. She had thick, straight brown hair cut in a fringe and a pair of determined legs that never seemed to get tired of carrying her. She had, as well, large, even teeth that were almost constantly revealed by her smile; and she talked most of the time, though she was only mildly disappointed if nobody listened. So far she had not appeared to notice the rather theatrical skyline visible from the front veranda.

It was drawn to her attention one day by her father, who appeared on the veranda after lunch, letting the wire gauze fly-door bang behind him. He stood, looking out toward the hills and rubbing his jawbone with the palm of his hand. After a few moments he said, "It's high time I did something about that boundary fence."

"What do you want to do to it?" asked Jane without thinking.

Mr. Thompson turned then and looked at her in some surprise. "Well, what one usually does to a boundary—check it."

"Oh, that," said Jane, and her interest waned. "I thought it might have been something interesting. If that's all you want, Bobby and I can do it for you. We've done all the others."

"That's the trouble," said Mr. Thompson. "I don't think you can. It's too far and too rough at the foot of those hills for you to do in one day."

For the first time Jane's mind registered what her eyes had been seeing ever since they arrived at Rosedale. "Does our boundary go among those *mountains?*" she asked in a high squeak.

"Course not," said Bobby. He had been sitting on the bottom step, drawing pictures in the gravel path, but he had not added a line since the conversation began. "It goes along the edge of 'em." He looked up then at his father. "Couldn't we ride it, Dad? Couldn't we?" and his voice held as much enthusiasm as he ever permitted himself.

Mr. Thompson shook his head. "Not on your own," he said. "But you can help me some day when I can find time to go."

There was silence for a moment while Bobby added another line to the gravel path. Then he said, without looking up, "There's that boundary rider's hut there. Remember we saw it that day? We could camp."

"Not on your own. Your mother would never allow it. When you're bigger, perhaps." He sighed, took his hat off the veranda post, and went slowly down the steps, and they both knew he was thinking that there was no end to the work to be done to a new place and how mean it was of the seasons never to wait for you to catch up.

During that afternoon Bobby was more silent than usual. But at dinner later on, he spoke. "Could we camp in that hut if we wait till Vincent comes? You said he was coming up in the May holidays. It's only two weeks off." And no one at the table could tell what an effort the suggestion cost him.

Vincent was the son of Mrs. Thompson's brother. Of all their cousins he was the one they saw most of and knew best, for he had been coming to them for at least one holiday every year as long as they could remember. He was two years older than Jane and would be fifteen when they saw him in May. He was one of those children who are classed by grownups as "satisfactory," and Vincent had been satisfactory all his life. Besides being rather above average at both work and games, he was, and always had been, a well-grown, good-looking boy. His shoulders were straight, and he held his chin well up, looking at people directly with clear, wide eyes. He was cheerful and friendly by nature and, unlike Bobby, who never even went halfway with his social contacts, had no trouble getting on with everyone he met. He was well thought of at his boarding school and held positions of authority, as Bobby well knew because he had been present at the school's Speech Day. Vincent was fond of both his cousins and made no attempt to patronize them, as he well might have. And he had recently given Bobby his outgrown bicycle, thereby earning, as Bobby readily admitted, his everlasting gratitude.

Jane had accepted Vincent as her hero from the first. She had never doubted that he was a person superior to her in every way, and she was happy that it was so. Unfortunately, she had made it clear that she also thought him superior to Bobby.

Bobby, though silent, was not ungenerous and no fool, and he readily acknowledged Vincent's superiority. When asked, he always said that he enjoyed Vincent's visits, and there had been times out west when he had genuinely felt a warm glow while introducing Vincent to their neighbors. He knew he was lucky to have such a cousin. He knew that the holidays were more interesting when Vincent was there. It was only in the last six months he had realized that the tranquil, peaceful feeling he always had after Vincent left for home was one of relief. So the suggestion he made now, if his family had only known, indicated a passionate desire to visit the farthest and most remote corner of the property.

Mrs. Thompson reacted swiftly. "What hut? Where? What do you mean? I didn't know you were thinking of camping."

Jane and Mr. Thompson explained the position to her simultaneously, while Bobby waited for his father's reply. This was what always happened, and no one thought it odd. At length Mr. Thompson said, "Yes, I suppose that might be possible. I certainly would like to see that boundary ridden. Of all of them, it's the most likely to need attention. It depends what your mother feels. What about it, Frances? Think they'd be all right camping if Vincent were with them?"

Mrs. Thompson now demanded a second explanation and, when it was given, sent one of her despairing looks down the table to Mr. Thompson and said, "It seems terribly cold to be camping just now, and I don't know what they're going to do about food. I'll have to get out a lot of warm underwear for them. But, yes, I suppose that if Vincent is with them, it will be all right." She ended on a note of almost placid optimism very different from the one in which she had referred to their underclothes.

Bobby knew then that the point was won and was not seriously concerned when his mother continued. "That boundary rider's hut is only an old shack, and it's right out in the scrub. If anything should *happen*—it's not as if they knew the country."

Mr. Thompson then pointed out that they knew the way there and, presumably, the way back, and beyond that all they had to do was to follow the fence. "As to anything happening," he said, "had you anything particular in mind? Man-eating wallabies, savage rabbits creeping up on them at night? Something of that kind?"

So next morning Mrs. Thompson started getting out the warm underclothes under the somewhat obscure impression that the sooner she did it, the warmer they would be.

After what seemed an exceptionally long two weeks, the term ended and Vincent arrived. He brought with him, as he always did, small gifts for all the family. This time they included a pocket knife for Bobby.

"For your birthday, too," he explained, for it was rather more lavish than usual.

Bobby looked at it carefully, turning it over in his palm. Then he thanked Vincent with sufficient enthusiasm and slid it into his pocket. There had been a time, many years ago, when he had been given the very first pocket knife he ever owned. He had wanted to show it off to the old fencer they then had, whom he much admired, and had taken Vincent down to his hut at a time when he knew the fencer would be skinning a couple of rabbits he had happened to catch. Bobby had been about to present his knife with something of a flourish when Vincent forestalled him by pulling out and offering his own—a much superior brand. Bobby's knife had not been shown that day nor for many days. It was an incident he had been unable to forget.

When they came to collect their gear, he carefully put the new knife in his drawer and strapped his old one onto his belt—not the old, original one, but another, well-tried, with the small blade sharpened to a wafer.

"Too good to take camping," he explained to Vincent.

It had been an exceptionally wet and humid summer, with so much rain that everywhere the grass was rank and sodden. All the creeks and dams were full, and as Mr. Thompson said, although they had numerous other troubles, they were not short of water. It meant, however, that the children must prepare for rain and must expect to find every creek swollen and perhaps difficult to cross. As, up to now, they had been accustomed to a much drier climate, they found the prospect pleasing and unusual.

It took them a day and a half to get ready, for Mr. Thompson said they must reckon on being away a week.

"A week!" said Jane. "Why, we could ride to Sydney in a week!"

"Well don't," said Mr. Thompson. "Please stick to the boundary fence. I said a week because you can't possibly take any longer. You'll probably do it in three days, but as I didn't go all along that fence myself when I looked the place over, I can't tell what difficulties you may strike. All I know is that it's pretty rough."

So they collected three gray blankets each from the cupboard where Mrs. Thompson kept the sleeping-out things, three chaff bags that they intended to stuff with straw and sleep on, three raincoats, the rather unnecessarily large number of underclothes and socks that Mrs. Thompson had put out for them, hairbrushes, toothbrushes, pajamas; and no pillows, because Vincent said they would use their clothes as pillows. Then they turned their attention to more important items: a frying pan, two billies, one for cooking and one for making tea, a tin plate, mug, knife, fork, and spoon for each of them, a small bag of flour because Vincent said bread would be too stale at the end of a week and he was pretty sure he knew how to make a damper, a flat cake of bread made of flour and water. Tea, sugar, cans of fruit, vegetables, sardines, one can of salmon as a treat for the end, butter, chops, and some cold corned beef completed the list.

When all these were assembled, Bobby added six boxes of matches and a can opener. Then he scratched his head, and his forehead wrinkled in a desperate frown. After a minute he said, "How are we going to carry all this on our horses?" Anxiety turned his voice into a hoarse squeak.

"Oh," said Jane, clapping her hand to her mouth. "We forgot. We were thinking it was the truck. Oh, aren't we stupid! Whatever shall we do now?"

Simultaneously, they turned to Vincent. In this appalling crisis he remained calm. "Well, I hadn't forgotten," he said. "But I had to wait till I saw how much it was all going to be. We'll have to take a pack horse, that's all."

"Oh," said Jane once more, but this time in a different tone. "Of course. So we can."

Bobby still wore his frown, though perhaps not so fiercely. "But we haven't got a pack horse," he said.

"Any old horse will do," said Vincent airily, "so long as it leads well. The bigger the better, really," he added after a second glance at the camping gear.

"Boxer!" said Jane triumphantly. "He's the biggest horse we've got, and he's awfully strong. He used to pull the plow when he was young, before Dad got the tractor."

"Before Dad got the first tractor," corrected Bobby. "He's old all right, but I dunno—he never would carry a sheep."

"Oh, well," said Vincent in a bracing manner. "We'll get him in and see. Perhaps we'd better ask Uncle Dick first."

Mr. Thompson seemed rather startled at the idea of his old pensioner being returned to harness but, after a minute's thought, decided that it would not be asking too much of him. Afterward he said to his wife, "He may slow them up a bit on the way there, but he'll never clear out and leave them. If once he'll take that almighty load, they can trust him to get there and back without trouble."

Jane and Bobby were to ride their own ponies because they were mountain bred and good on their feet. Vincent had reluctantly to give up the good-looking young horse he had been riding and content himself with one of the less handsome stock horses.

"Never mind, Vince," said Bobby, "he goes better than he looks." And if there was a touch of complacency in his tone, it was not unduly noticeable.

Once upon a time Bobby had taken comfort from the fact that riding was the one thing he did better than Vincent. Then one day when they had been skylarking, he had had the ill luck to fall off and knock himself unconscious on a stone. In the ensuing excitement, Vincent's pony had gotten away, and impelled by an anxious and tearful Jane, he had had to gallop home on Bobby's excitable and unreliable pony. They had gotten home in record time, jumping the final gate into the homestead paddock—a feat observed by several of the men who were working nearby. So Vincent's reputation for horsemanship was established early. Since then, by good luck, it had never again been put to the test. And no one but Bobby had ever suspected the truth—that the pony was bolting the day Vincent rode it and Vincent would have stopped it jumping the gate if he could. Certainly, to his credit, he had not fallen off, but it had been a near thing.

They got the horses into the yards the night before and gave them all a good feed. This was not strictly necessary, as Mr. Thompson pointed out, because there would be plenty of grass for them in the small paddock attached to the hut. But it seemed the right thing to do. Bobby's black and tan terrier-type sheep dog, Skyraider, also received three times as much dinner as usual. Puzzled but grateful, he consumed the lot. "The prisoner ate a hearty breakfast," murmured Mr. Thompson as he passed the kennel.

In spite of Mrs. Thompson's forebodings, for she habitually mistrusted the elements, the morning of their departure dawned bright and clear. There had been a slight frost, and the flats by the creek to the north of the homestead were silver-white. Bobby was the first to wake, but he lay quietly, though consumed with impatience, until Vincent rolled over, gave a snort, sat up, and rubbed his hands through his hair.

"Hey, come on, everyone," he said loudly. "The sun's up already."

Bobby slipped quietly out of bed and somehow contrived to get to the bathroom first. He was about to give his face its customary morning caress when he recalled that for the next week they would be far from bathrooms. Reluctantly, but with great fortitude, he eased his way under the shower. It was warm and, presently, as the soapsuds gathered upon him, he began to whistle through his teeth. Bobby seldom smiled, preferring to gaze out on the world with mournful gravity. But when he was happy, he whistled through his teeth.

The song and the shower ended abruptly when Vincent erupted into the bathroom. "Hullo!" said Vincent. "Having a *shower?*"

Bobby nodded. "Last for a week," he said succinctly.

"Oh, lor," said Vincent. "Then I suppose I'd better have one too." Without any noticeable enthusiasm he took Bobby's place in the steaming cubicle.

Damp, shining, and smelling of soap, they confronted the half-conscious daughter of the house. "Come on," they said. "You've got to have a shower."

"Why?" said Jane in affronted tones. "I had one last night."

"Last for a week," they said, adding with infuriating satisfaction, "We've had ours."

"Oh, dash," said Jane, who had intended a little light surface work with the toothbrush and something in the nature of a dry clean.

Having started her conscience working, they left her and went down to get the horses saddled before break-fast.

They did their own first, telling each other bitterly that they supposed they would have to do Jane's too, as all the omens indicated that she would be late as usual. She was, and they were just buckling the last strap when she arrived.

"Hullo," she said. "Haven't you done Boxer?"

Vincent, with a heart too full for words, gazed at her for a moment. Then he asked with studied courtesy, "Would you like me to answer yes or no?"

"Oh, you are an ass, Vincent," said Jane, delighted as she always was by Vincent's wit. "Thank you, anyway, for saddling Tinker. But why *isn't* Boxer done? He's the most difficult."

"Because we want to see how much will fit on our pommels and in our own saddlebags first."

They were able to stow away a good deal more on their own horses than they imagined, but nevertheless, now that the chaff bags had been stuffed, there was still a sizable load for Boxer. He stood, all fifteen and a half hands of him, in the only sunny corner of the yard, his big head hanging and one fringed hind hoof poised on its tip. He looked healthy enough and not exactly thin, but for one horse, even a large horse, he seemed to have more than a fair share of bones. In the course of time the spring had worn out of his bottom lip, so that it hung down loosely from his teeth, and he had a distressing habit of clapping it at intervals against the top one. His once handsome bay coat appeared to have rusted with the years.

He sighed as they slipped the halter over his head and, anticipating that he would shortly be asked to move, placed the resting hoof firmly on the ground. He came willingly enough to be tied beside the other horses.

"Nothing wrong with him," said Vincent cheerfully. "He's just what we want." Seeing Mr. Thompson approaching from the garden, he said more loudly, "I said he's just what we want, Uncle Dick."

Mr. Thompson placed his forearms on the rail and rested his chin on the back of his hands. Through the fence he surveyed their preparations. "Glad you think he'll do. Thought I'd just come down and see him load up. Your mum says breakfast's ready, but she won't mind it waiting for a few minutes."

It took them some little time to decide the best way to fix the load. They had no packsaddle and had to try a variety of methods before they found one that looked as if it would be satisfactory. As much as possible, they balanced the items so that approximately the same amount hung down on either side. The bags of straw went on first, and on top of them were laid the blankets, folded longways and thrown across. Then they strapped on the hardware, filling the billies with the more delicate provisions like butter, sugar, and flour. Finally, when all seemed snug and tight, Mr. Thompson found them an old piece of tarpaulin that had once covered a haystack, and they tied that around the load and under Boxer's belly as firmly as they could. Boxer himself took little interest in the proceedings, slightly to Bobby's disappointment.

"There," said Mr. Thompson when the last buckle was fastened and the last rope knotted. "That's gone on better than I expected. These scouts have their uses."

Vincent grinned amiably. One of the things that Bobby had been forced to admire about him was that although he did so many things well, he never boasted about them. Jane, who had only a few accomplishments and tended to make the most of them, found it more than praiseworthy.

As Boxer seemed either oblivious or contemptuous of his burden, they decided to leave him to get used to it till after breakfast. Before they started, he would be led around to see how it balanced during movement. Leaving all four horses tied to the fence, each with its nose in a feed box, they turned toward the house.

They had gone only a few paces when they heard a snort, a sudden tattoo of hoofs, and a sound like a percussion band.

Simultaneously they swung around. Boxer, his neck stretched to its utmost, was standing with his legs wide apart, at the full length of his halter. His wispy tail was clamped between his hind legs, and from the ground around him rose a cloud of dust.

"Thought so," said Bobby happily. "He's just noticed it."

Before they could reach the yards, he noticed it a second time, and with an agility that at his age was almost indecent, he flung himself into space. His hind legs went up, his head down; he bounded from side to side, thought better of it and half sat down, jerking his head back against the halter. This failed to produce results, and he took to bounding again. Every piece of iron-mongery on his back gave tongue and inspired him to even greater efforts. It was hard to see him for dust, but peering through the haze, they saw the moorings of the tarpaulin give way at last so that, impelled from beneath, it rose in the air like a parachute. Released now in their turn, the billies and the frying pan began to thrash and bang insanely. The tumult was deafening, and Boxer, beneath it, appeared charged with an electric current.

"Whoa!" cried Mr. Thompson in a voice of thunder. "Whoa, you idiotic old fool!" He climbed through the fence and rushed to the old horse's head, but it was too late. The billy on the far side flew off, apparently about to take orbit, scattering its contents of flour in the dust-laden air. A pound of butter fell beneath Boxer's feet and he trod on it.

Before the second billy could fly away, Mr. Thompson reached Boxer's head, grabbed the halter, and clung with grim determination to his ear. After a time he subsided, standing taut as a fiddlestring with heaving sides and flaring nostrils. His eyes still rolled wildly. Mr. Thompson spoke soothing words to him. At least, the tone was soothing, but the words themselves were insulting. Little by little Boxer allowed himself to be soothed. When he was calmer and while Mr. Thompson still held his head, they crept up and fastened the load again as best they could. At every tinkle of tin or sudden pull on a rope Boxer started nervously. But gradually, while Mr. Thompson softly called him unkind

names, he consented to consider the load on his back as a possibility. By the time they tied him up a second time he had become resigned.

"Think he'll be all right now, Uncle Dick?" asked Vincent.

Mr. Thompson nodded. "I'll come and get you started, but I don't think he'll give any more trouble. Once he has his little go he usually settles down. But I'm surprised. I'd have thought he was too old for that sort of thing. Must be the new spring grass coming."

"All that lovely flour and butter!" said Jane mournfully. "We'll have to get some more—and wash the billy. I don't know what Mum'll say."

Bobby said nothing, but as they walked up the path to breakfast, he whistled softly through his teeth, the sign that he was happy.

Mr. Thompson was right, and after breakfast Boxer behaved like a lamb—even, as Vincent said with excruciating wit, like a sheepish lamb. They repaired the

damage done, tried to think of all the things they might have forgotten, and prepared to leave. Mrs. Thompson came out to see them off, looking anxious and waving a packet of Band-Aids and a tube of disinfectant ointment.

"Take these, please," she said. "I shan't have a moment's peace unless I know you have them with you."

"Oh, Mum," said Jane. "We're all packed up now."

But Vincent put them in his pocket. "All right, Aunt Frances," he said. "And don't worry. I'll look after my troop."

Bobby gave him a quick glance from under sandy eyebrows. But if he minded being classed as Vincent's troop, no one ever knew, for he said nothing.

They got on their horses, and Vincent, at Mr. Thompson's request, took Boxer. "You can take it in turns to lead him later," he said. "But I want Vincent to start him off. Remember now, you're to go straight to the hut, unload and settle in, make sure there's water in that paddock for the horses, and get yourselves some dry fire-

wood. It doesn't look like rain, but in a season as wet as
this you can't tell. Jane is to sleep in the kitchen, and
you boys can shake down on that lean-to veranda. It's
pretty well sheltered. Go along the fence as far as you
can up to lunchtime the first day. Then the next day
you can find yourselves an easy route to where you
stopped the first day and go on from there. It may not be
as rough as I thought and you may finish in a couple of
days, but be sure and look at every inch of the fence.
You'd better make notes of anything that needs doing
and leave a stone on the nearest fence post. Clear?"

"Yes," said Vincent. "And how far along the fence are
we to ride?"

"To the end of the rough country on either side of the
hut. Up to where the paddocks have been fertilized.
You'll see easily enough."

"And, children," said Mrs. Thompson in a despairing
tone, "be *careful*." Then she added in a normal voice,
"And if you have to make notes, have you pencil and
paper?"

They had. And they said farewell and turned their
horses to the west. Mr. and Mrs. Thompson had just
turned away when Bobby returned at a brisk canter.

"What now?" asked Mr. Thompson.

"Forgot Skyraider," said Bobby hoarsely. And they
knew that he was happy to be going, for his voice only
became hoarse in moments of excitement.

Mr. and Mrs. Thompson watched them cross the horse
paddock, the two ponies walking briskly to keep pace
with Vincent's horse, and Boxer towering over them all
and spreading unnaturally on either side. Behind them
Skyraider, his whippy tail carried like a banner, trotted
busily from one side of the track to the other, as stones,

stumps, and tussocks claimed his attention. Every so often he looked up, perceived the distance widening, and raced after the horses.

"Nice to be young," said Mr. Thompson. "And now I'd better do some work."

TWO
HOME IS WHERE YOU MAKE IT

The children headed south toward the rough country. The sun shone warm on their backs, the paddocks around them were soft and deep with the new autumn growth of clover, and as they rode, the hills opened out in front. After the frost the morning was clear and sparkling.

"I like it here," said Jane with a sigh of satisfaction. "It's such lovely, explorey country. It has so many corners you never know what's around them."

Vincent looked at her in some alarm. "I hope you know what's around these corners," he said. "You're supposed to be the pathfinder."

"She knows," said Bobby. "Don't you, Janie?"

"Course," said Jane in some surprise. "I was here last week with Dad in the Landrover."

"She never gets lost," said Bobby comfortably. "Dad says she has a bump of locality."

"That's good," said Vincent. "You never know when we may need it." He turned to Bobby. "Like to take Boxer for a bit? The corner of the frying pan keeps rubbing my knee."

Bobby nodded and pulled over to Vincent. The halter was passed to him, and Vincent moved away. Boxer seemed unaware of the change, but beside him Bobby was scarcely visible. He looked up at the towering pack as one might gaze at a mountain peak. "I can put Skyraider up there when he gets tired," he remarked.

They rode on. The house and its surrounding yards and paddocks disappeared around the shoulder of a hill, the ground they trod became harder and more uneven, and trees and scrub became more frequent in the paddocks. Little by little they climbed into the hills. Every so often they went through a gate, and when they did so, the gate was flung wide and Jane and Vincent had to hold back until Bobby and Boxer were through. "Just as if he were an archbishop," said Vincent as Boxer surged past, his vestments trailing.

Finally, when the open paddocks had long since given way to stony, timbered hills and gullies, the track led them around a sudden rocky bluff, and they saw below them the boundary rider's hut.

It was built on the side of the creek that tumbled down from among the hills and here ran through a small valley that had at some time been cleared. It was well grassed, but except where a rather broken-down fence enclosed the paddock for the boundary rider's horse, it had been eaten short by sheep.

"The hut," announced Jane rather loudly, "is better than it looks."

This was heartening news, for there was, certainly, an air of individuality about it that did not necessarily spell comfort. The iron roof sagged here and there and leaned in an inebriated manner over the corner of the veranda where a post had given way. In place of the post were now two oil drums, one standing on the other and the roof resting on top. The front wall of the hut, sheltered from the weather by the deep veranda, was of weatherboard, but as far as they could yet see, the others were of ill-assorted pieces of iron, some corrugated, some not, and some frankly gasoline cans of antique vintage beaten flat. These were not painted and were, in fact, coming adrift here and there as nails had dropped out in the course of time. At the back a rusted iron chimney soared into the air, apparently having changed its mind once or twice about the direction of the vertical. One end and part of one side of the veranda was boarded in, after which, no doubt, the boards had run out.

Bobby regarded it in silence. To him it seemed the perfect holiday resort.

"Oh, well," said Vincent, "I think we'll manage all right here. It will be better than sleeping in the open if it's wet."

They moved on down the hill and before long found themselves at the gate of the little paddock. It was tied up with wire but seemed strong enough. Vincent got off and opened it after some trouble, and they took their horses through.

"I suppose we can let them go now, can't we?" said Jane. "I'm hungry."

"Take them up to the hut first and unload," said Vincent. "I'll just go around the fence and make sure they can't get out anywhere." He rewired the gate and set off in a businesslike way along the fence, for he realized his responsibilities and wished to leave nothing to chance.

When he returned, the saddles, saddlebags, and various articles of clothing were in a pile on the veranda and the three riding horses were tied to the fence. Boxer, with a patience that amounted almost to superciliousness, was allowing himself to be disrobed, and Jane was struggling frantically with one of the knotted ropes. "If we can't get this off," she said between gasps, "We can't have any lunch. All the food's under the tarpaulin." Driven by hunger she redoubled her efforts.

"Cunning is what is needed," said Vincent, "not force." He took the rope from her and quickly undid it.

"Oh, Vincent," said Jane, "I wish I was a scout."

Boxer was unloaded in far less time than it had taken to load him up, and when the last chaff bag slid off his back, he shook himself, hung his head, and sneezed. "Let them go?" asked Bobby, taking Boxer's halter.

"Yes," said Vincent. "The fence is right enough and there's heaps of feed. We won't have to worry about their starving."

"Water?" asked Bobby.

"Yes, water's O.K. They can get down to the creek at the far end there."

So Bobby went up to them one by one and let them go. Each horse as it was let loose wandered off through the grass, its head hanging, tail stretched out, and legs all wobbly at the joints until it found a suitable place to roll, and then plopped down in the inelegant way horses have.

Bobby watched them for a minute because Skyraider was known to bark at rolling horses, and it was a practice of which he disapproved strongly. However, this time Skyraider was far too busy investigating the possibilities of rats and rabbits beneath the hut floor to attend to the horses. Bobby returned to the hut to find Jane sitting cross-legged beside the pile of provisions and blankets, gloating like a miser at their quantity of gear. A can of sardines and a loaf of bread lay beside her right knee. So far preparations for lunch did not appear to have advanced much. "Where's Vincent?" he asked.

"Getting wood, I think," said Jane.

"Oh." He paused. "What are you doing?"

"Can't you see?" she asked indignantly.

"Seem to be having a rest," said Bobby, adding casually, "I'm hungry."

"Well, we can't do anything till the fire's lit, can we?" said Jane.

"Could eat some bread," said Bobby wistfully.

"We're having toast," announced the cook. "Go and get some wood and then we'll be all the quicker."

There is no arguing with cooks, so Bobby went.

He and Vincent each brought an armful of wood and then started to light the fire. At first Vincent was reluctant to use the piece of crumpled newspaper that Bobby produced, saying that a fire—any fire—should be perfectly easy to start with a few bits of leaf and dried grass. He only consented to take it as a foundation when Bobby said that he very much wanted it burned up to avoid mess and that just at the moment he didn't happen to have any dead leaves or dried grass.

They half expected that the chimney would refuse to draw, for it was obvious the hut had not been occupied for some time. Although the front door was not locked, they had had to lift it on its hinges before it would move across the floor. The small kitchen, though tidy enough, was full of dust and cobwebs. They gave up trying to open the window for fear it would carry away altogether, and they told Jane she would have to be content with her fresh air coming in by the door. The furniture consisted of a table, three wooden boxes, an iron bedstead that sagged badly in the middle, and a shelf that ran along the wall beside the stove. A rusty frying pan and a black billy with a wire handle stood upside down on the stove. A hurricane lamp hanging from the ceiling reminded them that they had forgotten their own.

"That's lucky," Vincent said, but Bobby climbed up on the table and tapped it with a stick. It clanked at them dolefully. "No kerosene," said Bobby.

"Oh," said Vincent. But later he added, "It doesn't matter really. We'll just have to go to bed and get up with the sun. Tons of people do it."

Surprisingly the stove did not smoke but lit up at once, and before long they had their billy boiling and their toast made. Jane blew the dust off the table, and they sat down with their mugs and plates. Outside, the autumn sunshine still beamed down on the grass, the air was fresh, and the birds sang; inside the hut little light penetrated, and the air was full of dust and the musty smell of forgotten places. But the three boundary riders sat at their meal in perfect content. This was sanctuary, this was home, and this was theirs alone for one whole week if they cared to stay. So far the expedition was a success.

When the meal was over, Vincent said, "We'll all wash our own things at the creek, and then we can spread out our beds and get in the wood. We'll get settled today so that we can start along the fence first thing tomorrow—"

He broke off and then said, "By the way, where is the fence?"

Bobby looked at Jane. Her eyes opened wide and her mouth slowly dropped. "I'm sure it's here somewhere," she said with great firmness.

"Oh, well," said Vincent. "I dare say we shall find it."

The creek ran only a short distance from the back of the hut, at the bottom of a short slope. It was very convenient for washing up.

"Oh," said Jane when she saw it. "But this isn't a creek; it's a full-grown river." And it was, indeed, a very well-grown creek. It swirled and rushed down the slope of the little valley, crashing and spurting against stones, bounding off the banks, and churning up little whirlpools of brown foam in all the eddies. Sticks and leaves swirled down with it, and it seemed determined to find sea level at the earliest possible moment.

"It's this wet summer," said Bobby. "All the creeks are like this now."

Later on that afternoon, when the wood was gathered and stacked on a corner of the veranda, the beds made, and the dinner bubbling on the stove, they came in and settled themselves for the evening. Jane had managed to sweep out all but the most elusive dust with a green branch, Bobby, burrowing with Skyraider in all the corners and crevices, had managed to find a small tin of kerosene, and the lamp now shone down on them cheerfully, if murkily, through its slightly smoked glass. Vincent, having made a final tour of the fence and horses, announced that all was snug.

Dinner was a huge success. Jane cooked the chops by the simple method of throwing them onto the flames, and they heated vegetables in some of the butter that had managed to escape Boxer's foot. Then they started on the big plum cake that was Mrs. Thomson's final gift. Finally, they passed around some toffee that Jane said she had noticed in a cupboard and thought they might need. Vincent looked at her in admiration. "Although you are only thirteen," he announced, "you are a most capable and thoughtful cook, and I shall give you a reference whenever you want one."

"Oh, Vincent," said Jane ecstatically, "will you really?" She relapsed into beatific silence, for praise from Vincent was something that she valued highly, and although she might have preferred a kind word for her beauty or intelligence, so long as it came from Vincent she wouldn't have cared if it had been for the size of her feet.

By the time they took their washing-up to the creek, the last of the daylight was draining from the valley. Far away, a hilltop, higher than the rest and crowned with tall trees, caught the last pale ray of sun. Two magpies hurried across the darkening sky to the trees across the creek, and in some distant valley a crow cawed its last, desolate good night. They walked back to the hut in silence.

From the hut's chimney a thin blue column of smoke rose straight into the sky. Somehow it was a pleasant sight, and Vincent said, "We'd better keep the stove stoked up for a while. It's going to be a frosty night. You can always tell when the smoke goes straight up like that."

"Means there's no wind, too," said Bobby.

When they reached the hut, Vincent rummaged among his baggage and announced he was going to brush his teeth while the light lasted. This was the sort of thing they found so advanced about Vincent. Left to himself, Bobby would have forgotten that he had teeth, and Jane would have so nearly forgotten that the little bit of attention she gave them would scarcely have been worth anything. However, in view of Vincent's admirable example, they began to search for their own toothbrushes and toothpaste, and Jane even went so far as to unearth a piece of soap.

Bobby had just succeeded in locating his toothbrush —oddly enough tucked into a hole in the padding of his saddle where the rats had gotten at it some months earlier—when Vincent returned. Jane said afterward that her first thought was he had met some terrible sight down by the creek bank in the dark; Bobby said he thought that Vincent had been suddenly poisoned. At any rate they both felt they were probably looking their last on their cousin, for Vincent's face was shocking to behold. His teeth were bared and his eyes screwed up and watering; his face was red, and he was grimacing frightfully. Every so often he coughed in a rather frightening way. Jane, her eyes on his face, tiptoed over to Bobby and took his hand. She felt that she required human contact. His bony fingers clutched her wrist.

Presently Vincent said, "Gibbe zubberdad dee shwiggly." This statement would have required a more advanced state of intellect than either Jane's or Bobby's if Vincent had not at the same time pointed a quivering finger at the stove. Slowly, with bulging eyes, they turned their heads. As they expected, they saw the stove, warm and comfortable, with its gently crackling fire. There was the billy of tea still on it from lunch, but nothing else at all.

"Yes," said Jane in a voice that quavered but which

she intended to sound soothing. "I see. It's the stove, isn't it?"

"Silly!" hissed Bobby suddenly. "He wants some tea. Get a mug."

Jane flew to the table, snatched her own mug, and filled it with the well-stewed tea. A considerable quantity splashed onto the stove and hissed angrily into steam. She carried the mug to Vincent and handed it to him at arm's length, backing away as he took it. They watched, spellbound, as he buried his nose in the mug, sucking and gobbling at the tea in an unnerving way. After what seemed an immense time he raised his head, wiped his mouth with his handkerchief, and put down the mug.

"Oh, gosh!" he exclaimed. "That didn't half sting. Thanks for the tea." His face had resumed its normal, pleasant expression. He was once again their cousin Vincent.

"What—what happened?" asked Jane.

"That beastly disinfectant ointment Aunt Frances gave us," he said. "I put it on my toothbrush."

When they had sufficiently composed themselves, Jane and Bobby made their own expeditions to the creek, but they prudently anointed their toothbrushes first and left the toothpaste behind. Jane was the last to turn in. Both the boys were in bed side by side on their chaff bags at the end of the veranda, their blankets wrapped tightly around them. They looked extremely comfortable. Skyraider was at their feet, curled up equally comfortably on Boxer's tarpaulin.

"Good night," said Jane from the doorway.

Two sleepy grunts answered her, and Skyraider beat his tail on the tarpaulin. She tiptoed into the kitchen.

Very soon she, too, was in her pajamas and had pulled
her bed out in front of the fire, for she had decided
against using the iron bedstead; it seemed to her to have
been designed for a person of unusual shape. She put two
more bits of wood on the stove, blew out the hurricane
lamp, and then squeezed her way into bed, carefully
avoiding untucking the blankets. She sighed, wriggled,
and relaxed. Now that the light was out, the night had
somehow invaded the kitchen, and the little softly flickering flames of the stove only served to deepen it. She became aware of all those silent hills, the gaunt trees, and
the big skyful of stars just outside the door. The inde-
finable, fresh smells of the autumn night flowed in to
where she lay. She heard the rush and gurgle of the
creek, still on its headlong journey to the sea far off in
southern Australia, the plonk, plonk of toads in the
muddy bank, one cheerful cricket somewhere just outside the hut, and a little farther off, the monotonous tear-
crunch, tear-crunch of their feeding horses. Almost immediately she dropped off to sleep.

THREE
THE BOUNDARY RIDERS

A couple of minutes later she was rudely disturbed by having the blankets dragged from under her chin.

"Hey, don't do that," she shouted, and grabbed at her disappearing warmth. Then she blinked. Vincent stood over her, fully dressed, and through the open door streamed the early morning sun.

"Sorry," he said. "But we've got to move you to light the fire." Yawning violently, she struggled to her feet and dragged her bed to the corner of the kitchen. When she had finished, it was scarcely disturbed at all; the little hollow where she had lain all night, still warm as she knew, remained. The blankets were only down a little way, the pillow of her clothes still folded. She glanced around. Vincent was on the veranda snapping up twigs. Bobby was nowhere to be seen. Very quietly she stepped in, sank down, crawled under the blankets, and pulled them discreetly over her head. The little gray mound moved once and then was still.

Vincent came in with his handful of twigs, pushed them into the firebox of the stove, and lit them. While they burned up, he whistled softly to himself. He glanced around the hut once, saw nothing remarkable, and continued to whistle. When the fire had caught to his satisfaction, he took the billy and went down to the creek to fill it. It was another morning as perfect as the one before. The frost on the grass had scarcely begun to thaw, but the sun was gaining warmth every minute. The magpies were making a tremendous noise in the trees round about, and farther down the creek a big weeping willow was just catching its first shaft of sunlight. Vincent squatted down and reached far out to get the running water in his billy. As he straightened up, he heard a scuffling and snapping of twigs and looked up to see Bobby and Skyraider coming down the hill at the back of the hut.

"Hullo, Bobby," said Vincent. "Where have you been?"

"Boundary fence," said Bobby, wincing slightly, for he strongly disliked his nickname, particularly when uttered by Vincent, for he thought it sounded girlish. "Skyraider thought he had a rabbit in a log so I went up after him. Saw the fence just over the hill."

"Oh, good," said Vincent. "Now we shan't have to waste time hunting for it. Come on, we'll go and have some breakfast. Jane's probably got it nearly cooked."

In happy anticipation they returned to the hut, their noses alert for the first hint of bacon. But all was silent. The stove was now going nicely, but there was no more sign of activity than when Vincent had left it.

"Funny," said Vincent. "I thought Jane would be dressed by now."

"I s'pose you woke her," said Bobby, who knew his sister.

"Oh, yes," said Vincent. "She got up and pulled her bed away from the stove so that I could light it. She must be still down at the creek somewhere having a wash."

"Didn't see her," said Bobby. "Besides, she doesn't like cold water much." His eyes moved carefully around the room and came to rest on the little pile of blankets in the corner. It looked peculiarly tidy for a bed lately vacated; also it seemed an odd shape.

"Never mind," said Vincent, putting the billy on the flame. "We can start the breakfast."

"She's the cook," said Bobby firmly, and walked over to the blankets. He bent down, grasped the side of the chaff bag, and with a quick heave rolled it over.

Muffled sounds came from beneath it. It rose up in the middle and undulated for a moment. Then the blankets flew apart and Jane emerged, tousled and red in the face.

"What did you want to do that for?" she said furiously. But Bobby was walking back to the stove, whistling through his teeth.

"But I thought you got up," said Vincent in a puzzled tone. "I woke you."

"Oh, well," said Jane with a defiant toss of her head. "I—" She paused and giggled suddenly. "I got back again." She grabbed her clothes and made for the door. "Shan't be long," she said airily.

It took her some time to live down this little lapse from grace, for her companions took care to parade their virtue all through breakfast, which, as they told her at frequent intervals, they had cooked entirely unaided and with great labor. However, when breakfast was over and Jane had staggered down to the creek with all the wash-ing-up, equilibrium was considered to have been restored and the unfortunate incident was kindly forgotten. And if, after that, she was heard occasionally muttering to her-self, the boys tactfully took no notice.

They all walked up the hill to inspect the fence, and as its line appeared to run in places where their horses would find the going difficult, they decided to put some lunch in their pockets and go on foot. It was something like nine o'clock when they set out.

The fence led them first of all down the far side of the hill, across the creek at a point where they were able to cross by jumping from rock to rock, and up an almost precipitous slope on the other side. They scrambled, slipped, and panted up the side of it until, after what seemed quite a long period, they reached the top.

"Do you think there's much more like that?" said Jane when she could get her breath.

"N-no," said Vincent slowly. He was peering down the farther slope where the fence now disappeared. "Not quite like that. It seems to be rather worse."

He was right, for the scrub on this side was a good deal thicker, having grown up at some time after a bush fire. Occasionally they were inclined to lose the line of fence as it plunged down among the undergrowth, from time to time changing course to avoid outcrops of rock and other places where it had been impossible to sink a post hole. Also, the tall trees were closer together here and prevented their seeing any distance ahead.

It was not, after all, very long since this part of the country had been first settled; perhaps a hundred years, no more. At a time when land was plentiful and white men were few, it was understandable that tracts of country as unpromising as this would be left rather severely alone. It was not surprising that landmarks and signs of habitation were generally absent. Only prospectors, looking for gold or copper, had penetrated very far into such a barren wilderness. Very probably no one except aboriginals had ever climbed many of the hills or penetrated any but a few of the more accessible gullies that lay to the south of them. Little by little farmers were pushing their way into the better-watered valleys, but it was taking a long time.

Vincent led the way, followed by Bobby who, being the smallest, carried the least weight, and Jane came last. Going downhill she found no trouble in keeping up, but when they were climbing, the distance between her and the others was inclined to widen. It was not that she weakened; it was simply that her legs, strong and serviceable as they were, were not long enough to reach from one boulder to another where Vincent had simply stepped and Bobby, rather more agile than his sister, had jumped. But she struggled on, determined not to ask Vincent to go more slowly.

Skyraider was the only member of the party who did not seem to find the going at all difficult. He scuttled through the undergrowth, enchanted with the multitude of new scents that he appeared to find under every log and beside every boulder. His tail was carried as jauntily as ever, his sharp little ears were pricked, and he bounced on his springy feet. Occasionally he flushed a rabbit, and he would disappear after it in a flurry of excited yapping.

Little by little they proceeded along the fence as it climbed and descended, crossed gullies and skirted precipitous slopes. There seemed to be no end to these timbered hills. The day warmed up, and the damp, leaf-strewn earth gave off a tangy smell, half mold, half eucalyptus. Once they heard a crashing in the bushes nearby and a wallaby bounded out, saw them, and turned and leaped off in great alarm, its crashing growing fainter as it disappeared down the hillside.

They did not forget to watch the fence as they went, and now and then Vincent would pull out his notebook and pencil and put on record a hole in the wire netting too big for them to mend, a rotten post, or a tree fallen across the wires. But on the whole they considered that it was in fairly good condition and probably had been put up after the fire that had caused the scrub to grow so thickly.

After what seemed a very long time, and long after they had run out of breath to talk to one another, Vincent looked at the sun and announced that it was past noon and they might as well have lunch. Thankfully, they spread themselves in the shade of a big yellow-box eucalyptus.

"What are we going to do now?" asked Jane when they had finished. "Are we going on, or do we go home?"

Vincent scratched his head. "I've been wondering," he said. "I don't see that we'll be able to ride to this point tomorrow if we go back now. We'd never get the horses here—at least, it would take longer than walking, and we don't want to walk it all again."

"No," said Jane with much feeling. "Can't we go on now that we're here?"

"I wish I knew how much farther it is to the open country," said Vincent. "If we go on, we'll be coming back in the dark."

"There's a moon," said Bobby, throwing the bone of a cold chop to Skyraider.

"Tell you what," said Vincent. "We'll go up the next hill, and perhaps we can see something from there."

So they went on, but once again, when they reached the top, they found their view obscured by trees. There was a particularly big, gnarled old tree right on the crest a little way from the fence that looked as if it might offer a better view. Bobby climbed it, and when he was no more than a small figure high up among the branches, his voice floated down to them. "It's O.K. I can see the paddocks now. There's not much more of this scrub."

"Righto," called back Vincent. "We'll go on."

In a few moments Bobby swung down from the lowest branch and, a little out of breath, landed beside them. "She's easy," he said. "Just a little way over there." He pointed ahead.

Much cheered, they set forth again. The fence still led them through some fairly rough country, and it took them longer than they had expected, but eventually the trees thinned out, the hills became less precipitous, and the fence led them out into green, rolling country where sheep and a few sleek Hereford cattle grazed.

"Oh, now I know where we are," said Jane. "This is the Back Creek paddock. Those are the steers Dad's going to sell."

But by this time the sun was low in the sky, the day was old, and in an hour or so the light would be starting to fade. Vincent tied his handkerchief to the fence.

"That'll show them how far we got," he said. "And now we'd better beat it for home."

For the first time it dawned on them what a long way they had come since they started off so fresh and ener-

getic at nine o'clock that morning. Suddenly they realized that their legs were tired and they were very hungry, for they had decided not to carry much lunch but to make up for it when they got back to the hut. They seemed a long way now from the hut and food. In silence they turned and began the long walk home.

The last of the sunlight still clung about the tree trunks when they reached their lunch place, and the sight of this milepost encouraged them. But Bobby announced that he wished he hadn't given his chop bone to Skyraider; he wished he had buried it for himself.

Shortly after this, the sun finally disappeared and the bush became very still and quiet. Skyraider now fell in behind Bobby and wasted no more effort chasing rabbits or searching for smells. No one spoke, for they seemed to have run out of things to say. Little by little the twilight deepened, the trees and bushes around them lost their color and their substantial daytime look, and became shadowy and vague. The ground began to play tricks on their feet, so that they stepped up when they should have stepped down and tripped over roots they did not know were there. In some odd way they found it a comfort to have the fence running securely and safely beside their right shoulders. Imperceptibly their pace grew slower, and each was wondering how long his aching legs would continue to carry him.

And now the sky changed from blue to pink, to greeny mauve, to a deep and glowing blue. One by one the stars came out, and it was difficult to see anything except what was directly in front of them, and only then as a thickening of the night.

Then, as they trudged doggedly on, a strange thing happened. A thin shaft of silver light appeared low down

between the tree trunks ahead of them, very gently and
subtly dispelling the surrounding darkness. Another shaft
appeared and another, and gradually the bush was flooded
with a pale and milky effulgence as the moon climbed
out of the valleys to the east, became entangled in the
eucalyptus branches, and eventually rode high and clear
in the sky above them. They were not troubled by the
darkness any more.

But, climbing slowly and painfully sometimes up and
sometimes down, they lost all sense of time, and perhaps
it was nothing but their hunger and the thought of those
soft chaff bags that kept them going. The moon was well
overhead and no one had said a word for perhaps an hour
and a half when they came to the top of the last low hill
and looked down on their hut, the little paddock, and
their sleeping horses.

"Never thought I'd see it again," said Bobby wearily.

When it came to the point, they found that they were
too tired to eat. They had a drink of water, shed their
clothes, and crawled beneath their blankets. Blisters,
scratches, and blemishes of all kinds could be counted
next day. Thankfully they closed their eyes and lost consciousness.

FOUR
WORLD'S END FALLS

Next morning no one showed any excessive enthusiasm about getting up with the exception of Skyraider, who rose at his customary time, visited each sleeper in turn, and finding himself universally unwelcome, lay down in the sun and from time to time amused himself with a little half-hearted scratching. The sun was well overhead when Bobby scrambled out of his blankets, dressed, and went down to the creek to fill the billy.

In due course the other two made their appearance, but their movements were languid and frequently accompanied by little yelps of pain as bruises, scratches, and muscles stiffened by the night's sleep made themselves felt. And when Vincent announced that as they had really done two days' work in one yesterday they should spend today regaining their strength and healing their wounds, they made no protest. In fact, Jane was frankly delighted and announced that in that case she proposed to spend the day alternately at meals or in bed.

So they pottered about, ate and slept, and every now and then told each other what a good job they had done yesterday and how difficult it was to get really lost if only one used a little common sense. In fact, they succeeded in making each other so overconfident that it was perhaps no wonder disaster, or something very like it, should eventually overtake them.

But that was not yet, and the day of rest passed pleasantly enough. The following morning they felt much refreshed and prepared to continue with the work. Their plans were as before; they decided to walk and take their lunch. The day was warmer with a few wispy clouds showing in the west. They made a good start and found that this time their fence led them for quite some time upstream along the course of the creek. On this side the going was easier; the scrub was not so thick, nor the hills so high. Sometimes they had glimpses of the hills rolling away to the south and occasional green valleys that looked remote and enticing. There seemed no sign of human habitation, although once or twice they thought they saw stock of some kind—it was too distant to see exactly what —in the small valleys. By lunchtime they had gone a considerable distance, and as they could see they had still some way to go before the boundary fence would take them out of the rough country, they decided to go back and do the rest of the job on horseback the following day. There would be no difficulty in getting the horses along this part of the fence.

It was on the way back that they saw the waterfall. It was at the head of one of the nearer valleys, and in the morning it had been in shadow. Now the sun shone full on what appeared to be a white and foaming cascade down a steep rock face. A cloud of spray hung at its foot, as if it ended in a sudden deep drop or broke itself on some sharp upthrust of rock. The depths were hidden and probably perpetually in shadow.

"Look at that," said Vincent. "Do you suppose anyone's ever been down there to have a look?"

"Oh, no," said Jane in a kind of breathy voice. "There's no sign of anyone here for *miles*. We're probably the first people who've ever seen it."

"Suppose the people who put up the fence saw it," said Bobby.

"Um," said Vincent. "But we didn't see it this morning, and maybe if they did the fencing in the summer, it wouldn't be flowing so hard. We *could* be the first."

"Oh, I do hope so," said Jane. "Do let's be the first to have seen it. Then we can name it."

"Right," said Vincent, striking what Jane thought rather a splendid attitude with his arm flung out. "I here pronounce we are the first to have set eyes on these magnificent falls, and we here name them—er—"

"Thundering Thora," suggested Bobby with a burst of inspiration.

But Jane, thinking this not nearly noble enough, suggested The Falls of the Magic Veil.

"Don't see anything magic about it," said Bobby with distressing logic.

Then Vincent said, "I would rather like to call them World's End Falls." And they all agreed that this name somehow had a fine dramatic ring and would do very nicely.

"And even if you can see a bit of the world over the

back of them," said Bobby thoughtfully, "people might think it's only the selvage."

As they turned to go, Jane said, "A pity we can't just pop over and have a look at them, now that we've discovered them and given them a name and everything."

"Too far," said Vincent, "and besides, we've got a job to do."

"Oh, much too far," agreed Jane sadly.

Bobby said nothing, but his eyes had a speculative look, as if they might have been measuring the distance.

That evening when they got back to the hut, they cooked themselves a large and satisfying meal, washed up at the creek, and then went to bed, as Vincent threatened an early start in the morning. It was a warm, still night, and here and there in the dark sky clouds hung idly, blotting out patches of stars. Down by the creek the frogs and toads were making a great noise as if they were saying farewell to summer.

"We'd better get some wood in before we go tomorrow," said Vincent from his blankets. "I think it's going to rain."

It was not long after daylight when they got up the next morning. More clouds had gathered in the night, and the sun had not yet climbed above them. It was still warm, and there was no wind.

"We'll try and finish the boundary today," said Vincent at breakfast. "We'll make sure there's plenty of dry wood before we leave, and if we get wet, we'll come home and dry off afterward."

So after breakfast they collected a large pile of sticks and stacked it in the sheltered corner of the veranda, tidied the kitchen, filled the billy and left it ready on the stove—"Because goodness knows how late or how wet we may get back," said Vincent, who seemed determined that they should end the day in some kind of discomfort.

Then they caught the ponies, who seemed mildly grieved at being taken away from so much rich, virgin pasture, saddled up, and started off, leaving an infuriated Boxer galloping up and down the fence and whinnying indignantly. His cries of rage became fainter as they crossed the rise and made for the course of the creek on the farther side.

They had gone for perhaps a mile when they came to a fork in the creek that they remembered from the day before. Vincent pulled up his horse, stood in the stirrups, and peered up the gully where the right-hand stream came from.

"This way," said Jane. "The fence is on the left here, remember?"

"Yes," said Vincent. "But I was just thinking that this might be the branch of the creek that has the waterfall in it."

"Oh," said Jane, "so it might." And she gazed ardently up the gully, too, as if she suspected that at any moment it might disclose the promised land. It did not, and she sighed. "What a pity we haven't time to go and see," she said.

"We'd find it easy enough if we had time," said Vincent with a confidence born of two days' successful inspection of boundary fences.

"Might have time when we finish the fence," said Bobby, and there was the faintest suggestion of hoarseness in his voice.

"Oh, well," said Vincent and sat down again in the saddle, "we'd better get on." He turned his pony's head in the direction of the fence, and they continued in a slightly subdued silence.

In perhaps an hour's time they reached the spot from where they had seen the waterfall. They stopped.

There was the valley, looking closer today in that clear, translucent air that precedes rain and makes even mountain ranges take great strides forward so that one is deceived by the apparent lack of distance between. They were deceived now.

"Not so far," said Vincent.

"Quite near, really," said Jane.

"Easy," said Bobby.

World's End Falls were not so spectacular this morning, but now that they knew where to look for them, they could see the long slide of water, the flashes of white spray, and the cloud that hung at the foot.

"I believe I can see where that fork of the creek runs through the hills," said Vincent. "And I'm sure it leads to the foot of the valley."

"So all we'd have to do would be to follow the creek up," said Jane.

"You couldn't possibly get lost doing that," said Vincent thoughtfully.

"Come on," said Bobby suddenly, kicking his pony smartly up the hill. "Let's get this old boundary fence finished." There were times in Vincent's presence when he found it necessary to assert his personality before it melted away, unnoticed by the other two.

It was not quite so easy as they expected, and they rode a long time before they came out into the open country and could pick out the boundary fence making its sedate way through a series of cleared paddocks.

"Well, that's that," said Vincent. "Now we've done all

this rough country for Uncle Dick." And he tucked away
his notebook and pencil. But the day was wearing on, and
they tied up their horses and sat down to lunch. From
where they sat they could see away out to the north and
west. It was all cleared, rolling country, very green and
pleasant after such a wet summer, with here and there on
sheltered hillsides clumps of trees, mostly pines, that indicated the position of the various homesteads. Sometimes
the little woolsheds (far smaller than the ones Jane and
Bobby were accustomed to) shouldered themselves up
next to the homestead as if they disliked being alone, and
sometimes they sat away out in a distant paddock in
sturdy isolation. It was a settled and bland countryside,
very different from the rough, wild ranges that lay directly behind them.

But they could also see, rolling up in great dark banks
from the western horizon, the army of clouds, of which
the ones of last night and this morning had been but the
advance patrol. Soon they would blot out the sun for the
day, and any sort of weather might lie behind that opaque,
black curtain.

"We'd better get a move on," said Vincent. "There's
rain in those clouds, and they're coming up quickly."

So they swallowed the last of their lunch, buckled the
straps of their saddlebags, and untied the horses from the
fence. Skyraider, who had lunched off three crusts and
half a tomato in a disgusted kind of way, bounced around
them giving little yelps of excitement. The ponies moved
about restlessly so that they had trouble getting on, but
at last they were all ready, and without any encourage-
ment all three ponies headed up along the boundary fence
and made off at a brisk and businesslike pace for the hut.

"They're in a terrible hurry to get home," said Bobby,

dissuading his pony from proceeding at an uncomfortable jog trot. "Must think it's going to rain any minute."

"Shouldn't be surprised," said Vincent. "It's getting awfully dark."

And it was not long afterward that Jane gave a little squeak and pointed to a big black bulge of cloud that now was almost on top of them. "Lightning," she said. "I saw it." To prove her words, the first long roll of thunder now broke upon them and went echoing away over the silent hills.

"Of course," said Vincent, and his voice was perhaps a trifle louder and more confident than usual, "The chances of actually being struck by lightning are very, very remote. Especially when you think how many people must constantly be out in storms and how few ever get struck. But one doesn't want to get actually *wetter* than necessary."

And they all agreed that getting wet was very disagreeable. The horses by now were frankly jogging with no noticeable effort of discipline on the part of their riders, and little by little the distance to the hut shortened. But it was obvious that one of the things that bank of clouds had been concealing was a storm, and no halfhearted storm either, for many more flashes followed that first sudden streak, and after each flash the thunder spoke again. Every now and again one or the other of the children would glance over his shoulder toward the south, for each had an odd fancy that empty stretch of country would somehow rise up and answer the oncoming storm. But the hills lay patient and unchangeable, the green of their timbered slopes now almost black in the dull light, and perhaps that was their answer and had always been their answer to the countless storms that had rolled over them from time immemorial. They might be temporarily wounded, floods might engulf the narrow valleys and scoop away great clefts in the topsoil, lightning-inspired fires might singe the timber from those great shoulders, but they were only temporary wounds, and in the course of time they healed. No storm however violent or noisy could really harm them.

Before long the rain began. They heard it roaring up the gullies and battering on the leaves before it actually hit them. When it did, it wet them to the skin in the first five minutes. Their raincoats were useless, for the water ran down from the brims of their hats inside their collars, it ran off the bottom edge of the raincoats into their boots, and it collected in little puddles in their saddles before

running away down the insides of their legs. The reins became black and slippery in their wet hands, drops ran down their noses and fell off the end, and frequently they licked the water off their lips, though the last thing they wanted was a drink.

The horses became sleek and shining, with flattened manes and tucked-in tails. They bent their heads, turned back their ears, and wrinkled up their noses, heading doggedly into the weather. Bobby's pony gave little snorts with each step, as if he were taking great care to prevent the water getting up his nose.

So engrossed were they in the difficult business of making progress that no one even looked up when they passed the World's End Falls. After a time, the thunder and lightning became less frequent as the storm moved away to the east. The first sharp downpour of rain eased, though now it turned to a steady, determined drizzle. Creeks that had been small trickles when they had crossed in the morning were now foaming torrents that wet the horses' bellies as they passed. Sheets of water were scouring out the hillsides, scooping the dead leaves into piles against rocks and logs and digging out channels where no channels had been before. There seemed a great deal of loose water about everywhere; in fact, far too much. Fortunately, the horses knew the way home, for the riders found it hard to lift their heads. They kept them bent, sheltering their faces and hoping for the best. Conversation languished.

They came to startled life, however, when Vincent's horse suddenly lifted his head, filled his lungs, and gave forth an ear-shattering whinny.

"He's heard Boxer," said Bobby.

"Oh, thank goodness," said Jane, "we're nearly home."

And home it seemed to them when they finally saw it, the ramshackle little hut still standing at the head of the small, cleared paddock. And in the paddock Boxer raced round and round, his bony head thrust into the air, his wispy tail curled over his back. Clods of turf flew from his hoofs, and they imagined they could feel the earth shake as he put down his great feet.

"Glad to see us back," said Vincent rather unnecessarily.

The creek had swollen enormously and was now lapping the horse-paddock fence. A great tide of brown water swirled down the middle of it. Fortunately, the hut stood out of harm's way on its little rise, but the tasks of washing and filling the billy would be much simplified now, for they had only half the distance to walk.

Stiffly they climbed off their horses and with awkward fingers unbuckled the girths. Their feet, swollen with damp, and chilly, did not take kindly to being stood upon. They slipped the bridles over the wet ears, picked up their saddles, and stumbled to the hut. The ponies shook themselves vigorously, blew their noses, and thought better of a roll on the sodden ground. They wandered off, picking at the grass as they went, while Boxer, coy and exuberant as a colt, cavorted beside them.

"We'll drop all our wet things here and go and light the fire," said Vincent, as he stepped, dripping, onto the veranda.

"Well, don't put all that water on the wood," said Jane anxiously, "or we'll never get the stove lighted."

"Oh, sorry," said Vincent, spinning around and spraying the blankets as he turned. For once he seemed very slightly at a loss. Jane did not notice it, but Bobby did.

His thin mouth became a little more compressed, and a spark flashed in his eye. He stepped forward.

"Best thing," he said crisply, "is to drop everything as soon as possible. Even if it's left in the rain, it can't get any wetter." And he shed his saddle, bridle, coat, hat, and shoes in a sodden little heap on the edge of the veranda. "I can't take *everything* wet off," he explained, "or I shan't have anything on at all." He gathered up an armful of sticks and stepped inside in his stockinged feet, and oddly, his expression was one of cheerful satisfaction.

Before long they had the stove lighted and the billy on and their clothes draped in a variety of ways over and around the stove. Steam rose up and filled the room. In their pajamas they prepared the supper, while outside the darkness fell and steady rain continued to beat on the iron roof. They felt very secure now that a few sheets of corrugated iron and strips of weatherboard stood between themselves and the weather, and it added zest to their appetites. It was a very large supper that Jane prepared that night, and it included the canned salmon. Afterwards, when they looked back on this last, fine meal, Jane said Something had told her that they must eat well. But at this moment her own tummy was the only thing that was telling her anything. They lit the lamp, stoked up the stove, and settled down to approximately three-quarters of an hour's steady eating. Then, gorged, tired, and contented, they stoked the fire for the last time, turned their clothes, which were steaming gently, and crawled into their blankets. Skyraider had not been forgotten during the meal, and Bobby complained from the depths of his chaff bag that Skyraider's hiccups were keeping him awake.

Long after the hiccups had ceased and all the camp was

asleep, the rain, little by little, eased off. The battering on the roof ceased, and if there had been anyone awake to listen, he would have heard an orchestra of drips, splashes, and trickles and, underneath all, the deep bass roar of the creek. One by one the stars came out and shone in a multitude of puddles and glittered on the wet rocks. The clouds folded back like a curtain, disclosing the great theater of the night sky. But by now even the horses were asleep.

FIVE
KEEP THE SUN OVER YOUR LEFT SHOULDER

It was clear and still when they woke. There was no wind, and the sun beamed down on a washed and amiable world.

"Well," said Vincent as they sat down to breakfast, "our job's finished."

"What do we do now?" asked Bobby. "Go home?"

"Oh," said Jane in a doleful voice. "Must we?"

"Suppose we must," said Vincent. But for once he did not sound very positive.

"We haven't been here a week yet," said Bobby.

"Three more days, actually," said Vincent.

"Seems a pity to waste them," said Bobby.

"But what can we do?" said Jane on a note that she usually reserved for despair and desperation.

And suddenly they all lifted their heads, stopped eating, and looked at one another. A great question hung in the air. Jane answered it. "World's End Falls," she whispered.

"I don't see why not," said Vincent in a sober, head-of-the-family kind of way. But his eyes were sparkling. "We could get there and back easily in the day. We know how to get there now."

"Oh, let's!" said Jane, clapping her hands together. "We may never get another opportunity—just the three of us."

Bobby said nothing, but as he took his plate and mug to the creek, he was whistling through his teeth.

Their saddles were still wet, so they decided to go on foot with their lunch in their pockets. This time they took a billy, which they carried in turn, and Vincent put a box of matches in his pocket. Jane was sure, later, that Something told him to do this, but Vincent got quite cross and said that things never told him anything, and he wouldn't listen if they did. He also said that he frequently put boxes of matches in his pocket, and it might even have been considered odd if he hadn't.

It was still quite early when they climbed the hill at the back of the hut. The creek was running hard, but it was no higher than last night and would probably fall in the course of the day. In any case they knew that it would never reach the hut. The horses, at the far end of the paddock, were lying in the sun looking very contented. The three turned their backs on this final acre of Rosedale and made for the creek and the rough country beyond.

Very soon they came to the fork that they had noticed yesterday. "This is where we turn off," said Vincent confidently. "I'm pretty sure it will lead us to the falls. But just in case it doesn't, we'd better notice the position of the sun."

They all noticed the position of the sun. It was where they expected to find it; in the east.

"Of course it will be more in the west coming home," said Vincent, who was not a scout for nothing. "We'll keep it over our left shoulders this morning and over our right shoulders this afternoon when we come home. I reckon we'll travel approximately southeast going and northwest coming back. If we remember that, the sun will keep us on course."

Much impressed by this display of cosmic calculation, they nodded. Nothing, they felt, would be easier. They proceeded happily, and it was as Vincent had said; the sun was over their left shoulder. They were walking, therefore, southeast. The morning was warm and pleasant, rather steamy after the rain but full of fresh smells. The birds were busy chasing the innumerable small insects that hummed and buzzed and clicked with a last frenzied ecstasy before the winter silenced their little orchestra. Skyraider flushed a little flock of grass parrots from a clearing near the creek, and they fled, chirruping, to the nearest branches. Another time two vivid red and blue rosellas swooped over their heads, and Vincent said it was a sign that they were in fairly high country, because there was an altitude—he couldn't remember what —that rosellas never went beneath. Another time a heron rose heavily from the reeds and flapped away uttering an unbirdlike croak. And always the magpies sang and caroled and gurgled to the morning.

This branch of the creek led them along a very twisting course, sometimes through steep gullies and sometimes (but not very often) through open glades where grass and ferns grew. Occasionally they would disturb small mobs of sheep that scurried away through the trees, so they knew that even if there appeared to be no fences, this country must belong to somebody.

There were farmers, poor but optimistic, who took up perhaps two hundred acres at a time of this unpromising but cheap part of the state in the hope that the sheep with which they subsequently stocked it would manage to survive among the scrub-covered hills and valleys. But the difficulty of finding them and looking after them, of keeping the rabbits in check—a job that a man could be fined for neglecting—and of maintaining such fences as there were usually turned out to be beyond all but the biggest-hearted, and no one had yet made his fortune here.

The morning wore on, and now they began to think they must be approaching the valley of World's End Falls. They tended to hurry at the approach of every bend in case it should reveal the valley, but every time it showed them only yet another convolution of the creek, yet another scrubby hillside.

"Can't be far now," said Vincent, and glanced up at the sky. "But we'll know better when the sun comes out again." The sun had slipped unnoticed behind an insignificant-looking little cloud.

They continued on, still untired, still confident that only a little more walking would bring them there. But the sun failed to come out, and now they noticed that the bush had fallen still. The insects no longer buzzed; birds no longer chirruped. The leaves of the trees hung quiet and still. The mood had changed.

"Funny," said Vincent. "Can't be much farther."

After perhaps another fifteen minutes' walking he stopped. "Tell you what," he said. "I'll just pop up to the top of this hill and see what I can see. You wait here."

So they sat and dangled their legs over a log by the creek bank and waited for Vincent. They saw some water beetles and one or two tadpoles by the bank, but the water was very dark and very still, and it was hard to see any distance into the depths.

"Even if we are wrong," said Jane, "we can always follow the creek back again."

"Um," said Bobby, who was kindly guiding a water beetle to the bank with a stick.

Presently a crashing of twigs heralded Vincent's return. "It's O.K.," he said. "I'm pretty sure I can see our valley over just a couple of gullies. I think we'll cut across. No sense in keeping to the creek when we know which way to go." Bobby opened his mouth to speak, thought better of it, and shut it again. Very slightly he shrugged his shoulders as he turned to follow Vincent.

They were glad to be able to leave the creek, for it had become a tedious guide. They clambered to their feet and followed Vincent up the hill. It was going to be even easier than they had imagined. When they reached the top, Vincent showed them the glimpse of green that he had seen. They agreed that it looked very like the Falls valley and was only a very short distance off.

"In any case," said Jane, "we'll know for sure at the top of the next hill, and if we find it isn't, we'll just go back to the creek again and go on."

It was quite a scramble to reach the top of the next hill, for its sides were mostly rocky bluffs and loose stones. They were certainly in rough country now. But, as so often happens, when they got to the top, they found that it concealed at least one and perhaps two or three hilltops still lying between them and the valley. Moreover, they could not now be quite sure that it was the right valley. It began to look too small, and Jane said it was the wrong shape.

Vincent very sensibly said they had better return to the creek when Bobby suddenly said, "Hey!" and pointed to the distant treetops. Ever since they had left the creek, the day, although they had not noticed it, had grown constantly darker. It was a long time since the sun had shone. And now they saw why.

To the south of them a dark bank of mist was rolling swiftly over the hills, blotting everything out as it came.

"Cold front," said Bobby. "Might have known we'd get it after that rain."

"It looks pretty thick," said Vincent, trying unsuccessfully to peer into it. "We'd better get back to the creek as quickly as we can."

They scrambled and slid and scuffled down the hill, and Skyraider raced with them. They climbed up the other side, puffing, gasping, red in the face. No one had breath for words. The air became cooler, moister, and little gusts now rattled the branches over their heads. They did not look up because they knew their way led uphill, and they were concentrating too hard on climbing. But if they had, they would have noticed that little by little the farther trees were receding into the mist. It was not as if they became merely hidden. It was as if they ceased to exist. Where there had been a tree, there was now nothing. It became a strange, white, silent world.

They kept together, and when the slope flattened out —for they could see nothing—Vincent stopped his

troop. "The top," he said, panting. "Now just follow **me** down the other side. The main thing is not to lose sight of each other." He crashed on down the hillside, and they followed. It seemed a long way down, but they all managed to reach the bottom together.

"This isn't it," said Bobby. "Where's the water?"

Their vision was restricted to a radius of about two yards, but certainly, in that small area, there was no water.

"Must be a bit farther on," said Vincent. "Come on."

They moved forward but very soon found themselves

climbing up again. Actually, they found that until the slope became fairly steep, it was difficult to tell whether they were going up or down.

"This is no good," said Vincent. "I think we'd better go back. If there's no creek, it can't be right."

Nobody had anything to say as they turned and made their way down and then up what they assumed to be the other side. They climbed until they could climb no more and then assumed they must be at the top—a top, anyway. Vincent turned to Jane. "What does your bump of locality say now?" he asked.

She screwed up her eyes, wrinkled her forehead, and for perhaps five seconds remained absolutely still. The boys stood still also, their eyes on her face. Skyraider, who had no notion of the seriousness of the occasion, came bounding up and put his feet on her thigh. Bobby quickly pushed him down and hissed at him, a sign, Skyraider knew, that his master was deeply displeased. He tucked his tail between his legs and sat down on as small a space as possible. Then Jane took a deep breath.

"Well?" they said.

She looked at them each in turn, her eyes round. "It's not working," she said. "It must be this mist. It presses around so close and makes everything sort of different. If only we could push it away just a little bit"—she made a futile gesture with her hands—"I'm sure I could tell— at least roughly."

"Perhaps," said Bobby, "if it was only roughly, we're luckier that it's not working at all. What shall we do now?" He looked at Vincent with a sort of challenge.

After a moment's thought Vincent said, "I think all we can do is to keep going down at different angles until we do find the creek. It must be here somewhere."

"And when we find it," said Jane with the faintest quaver in her voice, "we'd better go right back to the hut."

"Trouble is," said Bobby, who had been looking around on the ground as if he had dropped something, "which way did we come up? We've moved about so since we stopped I can't remember."

"Oh, this way," said Vincent confidently, pointing behind him.

But Jane shook her head. "No it wasn't," she said. "I'm sure it was from down that direction." There was a moment's silence.

Then Vincent took a breath. "Well, anyway," he said, "we needn't go down either of those ways. And, in any case, we may have to do it two or three times. Come on." He plunged off into the mist in a sudden hurry, and the others followed.

But there was no creek at the bottom there either, nor at their next descent. And the next time they reached the top, they rather nervously agreed that the top didn't look quite the same either.

"Never mind," said Vincent with a touch of desperation. "And if we happen to be farther along the top this time, perhaps that's lucky."

Down they went again, and it was lucky, for this time they came to the creek.

"Well," said Bobby, "*a* creek, anyway."

"I'm certain this is it," said Jane, bending down and subjecting what she could see of the water and a few moss-covered boulders to a minute inspection. "Look, Bobby, there are the water beetles."

"Hum," said Bobby, bending down in a skeptical kind

of way beside her. "I never could recognize the face of one water beetle from another."

"I think it's our creek, all right," said Vincent in the heartiest tones he had used for some time. "Question is, which way do we go?"

"This way," said Jane positively, and pointed to the right.

So they set off along the creek with a brisk step, stumbling and tripping as they went, for the mist was still very thick about them, and if it had not been for the ground beneath their feet, they might have thought they were walking along the edge of nowhere. Little globules of water formed on their hair and clothes, so that before long they all became faintly tinged with the silver gray of the mist. They could feel the air wet on their faces, and every so often a branch would loom up out of the void and slap them as they passed. Except for the companionable gurgle and splash of the creek, the day was still very silent. Jane kept remembering little landmarks as they passed; a rock here, a bit of scrub there, and more and more their confidence returned—so much so that Bobby suddenly stopped dead and said, "Hey! What about lunch?"

During this anxious time none of them had given it a thought. Now they realized they were starving and sat down to it forthwith. They were about to boil the billy, but Vincent said he thought they had better not waste the time. He thought it must be getting well on already in the afternoon.

"Pity we can't see the sun," said Bobby. "We could tell if it was on the proper shoulder."

It did not take them long to finish all they had, and

Vincent made them hurry on so that they should be home before dark.

"It'll get dark pretty early tonight," he said.

They continued on down the creek, and now they thought that perhaps the mist was receding a little. They thought they could see farther ahead, though now it seemed undecided whether to be mist or drizzle. It was definitely wetter. Jane no longer announced familiar landmarks, and they walked, still purposefully but silently, for some time. Then Vincent said, "Are you sure, Jane?"

"No," said Jane in a small voice.

"Better go on, all the same," said Bobby. "Too late to go back now, and if it is right, we still want to get home before dark."

So they went on, but their steps were less lighthearted and their pace began to slacken. Bit by bit the mist cleared, and bit by bit the rain began. They could see the trees around them quite clearly and the hills rising up on either side. It was still hard to know whether they were on the right track; every hill, every twist of the creek looked so much like the last. It could be right, or they could be walking with great determination in totally the wrong direction. There was nothing for it but to continue.

It seemed to them they had covered miles and miles when Vincent, who led the way, suddenly stopped and looked upward. After a minute he said, "Thought so. I believe it's beginning to get dark."

They looked at one another and said nothing. They were very wet now and no longer as warm as they were. "Better keep on," he said soberly, and without a word they turned and continued. Perhaps the next bend would show them familiar country.

But it didn't. Nor the next; nor the next. And it was clearly growing darker. There was still no sign of the sun, and they had no means of telling in which direction it was setting. It might have been anywhere in that featureless half-light.

At length, when walking had become almost as difficult as it had been in the thickest of the mist, they turned a corner and saw—not the fork of the creek and the boundary fence that they had hoped to see but a little valley opening out among the hills, green and cropped short by sheep, and along the creek bank a number of old, gnarled casuarinas, their somber branches held out protectively over the water below.

"Now we know we were wrong," said Bobby eventually.

They sat down. Somehow their knees suddenly failed to hold them. This was not home; this was not even the valley they had hoped to find. It was far too small, and there was no sign of any waterfall at the far end. They were lost, and they knew it.

Vincent said slowly, "I think we'd better stay here the night. We won't do any good trying to go farther."

"Wh-where shall we sleep?" asked Jane, and if there was a sob in her voice, who could blame her? They were wet and cold and hungry, and it seemed a cold, wet, bleak place to spend the night. In silence they wandered up and down the creek.

There were many signs of sheep, but there were no sheep here now; they had already gone to the higher slopes to spend the night.

"Perhaps if there are sheep, there might be a shed,"

said Bobby hopefully. But there seemed to be no shed and no sign of human habitation anywhere.

"We'll have to try and scoop out holes among the roots of these trees," said Vincent when they had looked everywhere they could. "If we make them on the leeward side and then build a nice fire, we might be able to keep fairly warm." The way he said it sounded quite homey, and Jane cheered up a little.

"It's nice, soft sand where the trees are, anyway," she said hopefully. She bravely did not add, as well she might, that the sand, like everything else, was getting damper all the time.

There was a group of about half a dozen she-oaks fairly close together on the edge of the creek bank. At one time the creek must have come almost up to their roots, but apparently fairly recently, and probably as a result of the heavy rain there had been in the summer, it had now carved out a new bed for itself a little farther off, and a considerable expanse of sloping sand stretched from the foot of the bank to the creek. It had also undermined the bank at some points, so that a great number of roots hung down exposed until they reached the sand. The outer tree of this group had succumbed to the undermining and had collapsed into the creek, its great trunk stretched across the spit of sand and its tortured roots writhing in the air. But where the roots had torn away from the bank, there remained a hollow partly roofed over by other roots still attached to the soil above and protected in some measure by the roots of adjoining trees. It was not exactly a commodious shelter, and it had the disadvantage of being intersected at various points by broken roots too thick to bend or break. However, it offered moderately good possibilities of protection, and here they decided to set up their camp.

Vincent organized. "Jane, you see if you can find enough dry sticks to light a fire. Bobby, you and I will dig out among these roots as much as we can. If we can only dig in far enough, we ought to be out of the rain a bit, anyway."

They set to work; the boys dug and Jane collected. Vincent stopped to help her light the fire as soon as she had found enough sticks to do it. He said that once they got the fire going, they could dry off more wood as they wanted it. But they found that they had to make a shelter for the fire as well as for themselves. The rain was now coming down too heavily to light it in the open. Eventually they got it going in a little hollow under one of the living roots.

"I hope it doesn't do too much damage to the root," said Vincent. "But I don't think we can be too fussy about that tonight." He returned to his digging, and Jane continued to lay in a supply of sticks for the night. It was difficult to know where to put them when she had found them. But she did the best she could. The boys, in the meantime, were finding that it was reasonably easy to dig out under the bank, and they managed to make two holes that were at least partly protected from the rain. One hole, where two roots bulged more widely apart than usual, was fairly big. The other was only just big enough for one.

"I hope the bank doesn't decide to come down on top of us," said Vincent, for it did seem to hang rather precariously over the top.

"We'll easily crawl out," said Bobby.

When the holes were finished, they broke some

branches off the dead tree and laid them across the roots attached to the top of the bank. As a roof, they were not very satisfactory, but they were better than nothing. It was now almost night. The fire, mercifully still alight, was belching forth a lot of smoke from the wet wood, but it managed to produce, also, a small, bright flicker of light that was immensely reassuring. It was not, actually, particularly warm, and as they had to be out in the rain if they wanted to be anywhere near the fire, it was not very satisfactory for drying their clothes.

Now was the time when they would ordinarily be having supper, and they began to feel hungry. But they had eaten their last crumb for lunch. There was nothing to do but crawl into their holes. They did so, and Skyraider, who was also wet and not as jaunty as he had been, crawled in with them. Jane was allowed the smaller cavity on her own, and the boys and Skyraider crawled into the other larger one on the other side of the dead tree. They tried to make themselves comfortable and might have succeeded better if their clothes and the sand had not been wet and if it were at all possible to avoid the raindrops that came through the overhead roots. The temperature had fallen considerably about the time the rain began, and now that they had stopped moving, they began to feel cold. No one had said anything for quite a time when Bobby spoke for them all. "It's going to be a long night," he said.

SIX
HUNGRY AND TIRED

For a long time none of them slept at all. They were too wet, cold, uncomfortable, and, if the truth must be told, dismayed at their predicament to think of sleep. Instead, they lay curled up and watched the fire, and from time to time one of them would get up and throw on a few more sticks and then crawl, shivering, into his hole. They could see the raindrops glistening in the firelight and hear them pattering on the sand all around, but beyond the little radius of the fire they could no longer see anything. They tried to forget that they were surrounded by strange and lonely hills, that tomorrow they would have to face the problem, empty and weary as they would be, of finding their way home. They tried to forget that they were cold, uncomfortable, and hungry, and they closed their eyes and tried to sleep. It was a long time before they succeeded, but at last, one by one, they lost consciousness as the long day, the climbing, and the anxiety began to tell on them.

After perhaps two hours Jane woke. It was still pitch dark and the rain was still falling. She doubted very much whether she had ever been asleep at all. But all her limbs ached, she was perished with cold, and her teeth chattered. She opened her eyes and saw that the fire had fallen to a small glow. She forced herself to crawl out, but moving was painful, and it made her feel colder than ever. She put some wood on the fire, noticing that the pile was going down rather quickly, and started to crawl back into her hole. The prospect of curling up in that cramped, cold place for another endless period was not inviting. But she could not stay where she was. She hesitated, peered into the boys' hole, could see nothing, and burst into tears. Through chattering teeth her sobs sounded strangely. There was a small movement, a couple of stifled grunts, and in the light of the now faintly revived fire, she saw Bobby emerge on his hands and knees. His teeth were chattering too, and he shivered as he climbed painfully to his feet. But he took her firmly by the hand and pulled her toward their hole.

"Come on in with us, Janey," he said, and for all the chattering teeth and a tendency to hoarseness, his voice was reassuring. "We're all cold, but we'll be warmer together, and it won't be long now till morning."

So Jane somehow climbed into the other hole, and between the three of them and Skyraider they managed to generate a little warmth. Vincent, she found, was awake, but too cold to move. This hole was more comfortable than hers but inclined to be wetter. Vincent naturally, being bigger, tended to take up a great deal of room, and from time to time they all had to move because

he said one or other of his legs was getting cramped. Jane
and Bobby knew that cramp is very painful and did their
best to make room. But really, there was no getting away
from the cold, the discomfort, and the wet, and stoically
they put up with it.

Fortunately, it is very difficult indeed to stay awake
all night, and one by one they dropped off to sleep again.
The fire burned on, grew lower, and eventually went out.
A small breeze stirred and blew some of the branches
off the top of them, and once Skyraider got up, trotted
outside on his own affairs, and returned, sneezing, to curl
up in the small of Bobby's back. But this time none of
them woke. They were exhausted, and for the time being
their bodies had given up.

Gradually the dawn broke on a gray, wet world, and
the cold grew worse than ever. It woke the three sleep-
ers, and Vincent sat up. His face had somehow become
thinner in the night, and it was very dirty. Its usually
cheerful expression was quite absent, and his mouth
turned down at the corners. His sleep did not appear to
have refreshed him. Neither did Jane's, for she groaned
as she moved and sat up. She yawned and rubbed her
face.

"Thank goodness the morning's come," she said. "I
thought the night would never end." She rubbed each
arm with the opposite hand. "Oh," she moaned, "I feel
terrible."

Bobby had not moved. He lay curled up beside them,
but his eyes were open.

"We can get up now, Bobby," said Jane, prodding him.

Between clenched teeth Bobby said, "I can't. I'm terribly stiff all over." He certainly lay crunched up in a
funny, tight way. Jane, in a sudden wave of alarm, began

to rub his arms and legs. After a minute Vincent helped her. Bit by bit they got them moving again. Bit by bit a little color came back into his shriveled gray face. After a while he got stiffly to his feet. They noticed with some relief that his legs appeared just capable of holding him up.

"I'm all right," he said, still between clenched teeth, and they realized he was deathly cold. "I'll be fine when we start moving; warm me up."

"Who let the fire go out?" said Vincent, who had just noticed it.

"Oh, Vincent," said Jane, and her bottom lip quivered. "Nobody *let* it. It just went. What shall we do?"

Vincent searched through his pockets and produced the box of matches. He opened it and looked at them carefully, muttering and poking the matches about with his finger. Then he looked up. "We've got two dozen matches," he said. "After that we won't be able to light a fire any more. But I need a hot drink, don't you? I think we ought to boil the water. We'll light a fire now."

They got what dry leaves they could, though nothing was really dry any more. Jane found some dead grass under a stone, which she said *must* be dry, and with these and a few twigs they tried to light the fire. The first match lit a leaf; it flared up, made a little greenish smoke, and went out. The second match turned the dry grass black but did not succeed in producing a flame at all. The third lit a few more leaves, and these all burned together for a few seconds in a more promising way. Vincent put down the box of matches and leaned down to blow the flame.

For a time the fire showed signs of lighting properly, and Vincent and Jane fed it, nursed it, breathed on it, and if they could, they would have burned for it. But the conditions could hardly have been worse for lighting a fire, and this short spurt did not last long. The flames retreated, turned lazy, and eventually went out. They tried to kindle the red glow that remained, but every little twig and leaf they put on it seemed to discourage it more. It grew fainter and fainter, clouds of greenish smoke billowed up, but even these lost heart after a time, and in the end they had to admit the fire was out.

"Oh, well," said Vincent, getting to his feet. "We'd better light it again." He reached out his hand for the matches.

"Better not," said Bobby quickly through chattering teeth. "Can't afford to waste any more. Better wait till the wood's dry enough."

"But I nearly got it lighted that time," said Vincent, picking up the matchbox.

Bobby shook his head again. "Not sensible," was all he said this time, but his eyes, looking full into Vincent's showed no signs of wavering. Except that his body was shivering with cold, he stood quite still.

Vincent's face showed the first sign of pink that day.

"We can spare another couple of matches. There are still plenty." He leaned forward, but oddly, Bobby's gaze still held him. Halfway to pulling out a match, he hesitated. Then he felt a tug at his sleeve.

"I can't find any more dry leaves," said Jane. "Everything's sopping wet." Her face, with its streaks of mud and charcoal, was woebegone and forlorn.

The moment passed, and perhaps it was only chance that the match was not struck. Not even Vincent could have said. He took a deep breath. "Very well," he answered. "We'd better leave it for the present. Come on.

We can't stay here. Even if we never find our way home, we'd better try to find some shelter somewhere." It was the first time such a thought had been spoken, and it sent their spirits to their boots.

They decided to make for the highest hill they could see, in the hope that they might find some familiar landmark from the top. But they were a long time getting there, for their speed today was about half what it had been yesterday. However, the walking warmed them up a little, and for a time they felt somewhat revived. But when they reached the top, their hopes were once more dashed. The clouds hung too low for them to see anything but the surrounding rugged hillsides. All they could discover was that from here the country looked rougher and more desolate than ever.

"Shouldn't think even a sheep could live there," said Bobby.

It was even too overcast for them to guess at the direction of the sun. They had, by now, hopelessly lost their bearings and might just as well go one way as another. But Vincent said, "Of course, we ought to stay just where we are and not move at all till they find us."

"Who?" said Bobby. "Nobody's looking for us yet."

And then they realized that they would not be missed for another two days. Perhaps after that, when Mr. and Mrs. Thompson had waited for the rest of the last day, paid a visit to the hut at the end of the week, and then perhaps made a few inquiries of their neighbors, somebody might start searching.

"We'll be awfully hungry by then," said Jane in a high, thin voice. "I'm hungry now."

"So am I," said Vincent. "I wish we hadn't eaten our lunch."

"Funny to think all that lunch was inside us yesterday," said Bobby in a dreamy voice. "Seems to have gone now."

"Another thing we ought to do," said Vincent with a spark of his old energy, "is to light a fire. People will see the smoke."

This was one of the very few occasions on which Bobby was ever known to smile. His tired eyes twinkled; his thin mouth stretched into an unaccustomed grin. "How?" was all he said.

"Well, I think we ought to go on," said Jane, and the boys realized with some alarm that she was near to tears. "We're all cold and hungry, and if we stay on this freezing hill much longer, we shall probably all die." She dug her knuckles into her eyes and in a rather muffled voice added, "Mummy wouldn't like it."

"Oh, heavens," said Vincent. "What are we going to do, then?"

"Come on," said Bobby. "We got to find some shelter. We've got to keep alive somehow till it clears and then find our way home. Let's try this steep country. It'll be warmer down there in the gullies, and we may find some caves or something." He stumbled off down the hill, and without a word the others turned and followed him.

Perhaps the less said the better about that day. When they set off from that hilltop under the low, concealing clouds and in the drizzling rain, which by now had started again, they understood for the first time just how serious their position was. This was wild country; there were large areas without a human habitation; even the fenced-in portions were seldom visited, and although they had seen signs of sheep, they might easily have broken through some tumble-down fence, and this might not even be a fenced-in portion. They could not see where to go, and for at least two days nobody would miss them. It had not before dawned on them that they could be in any actual danger. They, like most people, were unaccustomed to the thought of personal danger, and at the most they had foreseen a period of discomfort. At last they knew it was a good deal more serious than that. Unless they were lucky enough to run across a road or even a fence, they had only their own wits to depend on, and wits are not at their best when one is cold, tired, and hungry.

The day stretched on into eternity. They climbed down gullies, up hillsides, over rocks, through scrub that scratched their legs, and across very occasional grassy hollows; and nowhere did they see a sign of shelter or a sign of human life. They felt they had traveled hundreds of miles, but they did not know how slowly they were now walking. From time to time one or the other of them would complain of a pain in the tummy, and then they would stop and rest. But after a time they all had a continuous pain in the tummy, and they could not rest forever. They thought they might have caught pneumonia or been poisoned by one of the pools from which they had drunk, and imagined themselves ill and helpless in this desolate wilderness. They did not know that their illness was nothing worse than hunger. They had never been as hungry as this before.

Only Skyraider retained a vestige of his old high spirits, and he was lucky enough to breakfast (or it may have been lunch, for they really didn't know) off a fat green frog that he found in some reeds. But one frog, however fat, does not last long. Soon he gave up making excursions into the bush on either side. He kept to the track behind Bobby's heels, and his tail descended to half-mast.

Bobby was still leading the way, for he had started off first and it had not seemed worth anybody's while to pass him. They were beginning to think it did not matter which way they went. They had been traveling in silence for quite some time when Bobby suddenly stopped dead, bent down, and picked something up. He looked at it carefully, wiped the mud and leaves off it, and held it up for inspection

"Look," he said hoarsely.

It was the iron head of a shovel—bent, broken, and rusted, but still the head of a shovel.

"Somebody's been here before, anyway," said Vincent. "Let's go on. We might find a track or something."

They continued in the direction they had been going, and Bobby carried the shovel head. It was quite useless, but they found it comforting. It was nice to know that someone at some time had once passed this way. Now, instead of keeping their heads bent and their eyes on the ground in front of them, they straightened their backs and looked about, searching eagerly for anything that might show them what that person had been doing here and where he had been going.

"What would he be wanting to dig for?" said Jane.

"Post holes, perhaps," suggested Vincent. "So we might see a fence soon."

Bobby studied the shovel head for a minute and then said, "Don't think so. Wrong shape for a post-hole shovel."

"Perhaps he was going to dig potatoes," said Jane with her first giggle in twenty-four hours. But there was a touch of hysteria in her voice.

For some time they saw no other sign of human life

at all. Then this time it was Vincent who suddenly stopped and said, "Wait a minute." He pointed to where the scrub grew thick along the base of the steep and almost clifflike hillside on their right. "Isn't that a track through the scrub?" he asked.

They all looked carefully. There certainly did seem to be a break-through between the bushes. It was overgrown and had obviously not been used for some time, for it was thick with leaves and fallen twigs and twisted lengths of bark. But it was a gap and had the appearance of not being a natural gap between the bigger and more firmly rooted plants.

But they were cautious now after many disappointments, and Jane, after a little ejaculation of surprise, said carefully, "It's probably only another of those sheep tracks we saw before."—for there had been one or two occasions when their hopes had been raised by these little tracks that petered out after a few hundred yards.

Bobby studied it carefully, squatting on his now rather wobbly legs, and then said, "Looks like an old track all right, but where would it go, up in that great wall of stuff?" And it did seem rather pointless to make a track that led straight to the foot of a slope like the side of a house.

"Let's try it and see," said Vincent, and he led the way toward the patch of thick undergrowth and followed the gap in between it. The scrub did not go far up the hill, for the steepness made it too difficult for the roots to cling in the sandy soil. Here and there were big trees that had managed to gain a roothold between rocks and now clung grimly to their position, and for the rest it was mainly tussocky grass, a few precarious saplings, lichen, and trailing strands of purple sarsaparilla.

"Now where?" said Vincent as they emerged from the scrub.

"This way," said Bobby, and his voice was hoarse again. He turned to the left and led the way along beside the bushes. The other two could see then that there was a little indentation in the ground running along the side of the hills. It no longer had the appearance of a sheep track; it might now almost have been made by a pair of wheels, though what kind of catlike vehicle would be climbing these slopes they had no idea. It was not always easy to follow, but Bobby did not hesitate. He moved steadily on, his eyes busy with the ground in front of him, and the others followed, not daring to speak for fear he should lose the thread. It was rather like reading a letter written in a difficult handwriting. It is all right if you keep going, but once you stop, you have lost it and have to go back to the beginning. Bobby never stopped, and they wondered where his thin legs had suddenly found their new strength. Both Vincent and Jane were now suffering with limbs that had begun to tremble and with heads that had a tendency to turn dizzy from time to time, and they found that it required a lot of effort and concentration to keep going at all. But no one wanted to stop. They said nothing and went on.

They were rising a little now, crossing the hill diagonally and making a fairly straight course between the many outcrops of rock and loose boulders that littered the slope. Once or twice Bobby hesitated, scratched his head, pondered, and then continued on once more, and so far they had not lost this faint shadow of an ancient track. They could see the bottom of the gully some way below them, and little by little they made their way around the shoulder of the hill, branching off from the main gully into a smaller subsidiary one. None of them had any idea of the time of day. By their reckoning it should have been midnight long ago, but they prayed now that it might not get dark too soon. They dreaded the coming night, and it would be heartbreaking if they had to stop now that they seemed to be going somewhere at last. But so far, although the day was dark and there was no sign of the low clouds lifting, it was no darker than before. The drizzle had eased off to a light mist, and while they walked, they were able to keep the worst of the cold at bay. Their greatest trouble was their clothes, which by now were quite wet through and had a tendency to rub them in places like the back of the knee, under the collar, or around the wrists. None of them had ever had any idea that it was possible to be as uncomfortable as they were now.

But the track was still discernible, and they followed it with hope in their hearts that for the moment banished all other thoughts. They could see now that some distance ahead a great bluff of rock jutted out of the hillside and ran into the gulley below, so that the little creek that wound its way down among the rocks had to take a big sweep to avoid the bastions of stone that the hillside here flung out into its path. As far as they could see, the track led fair into the middle of this great jumble of rocks. It was as if, seen from this distance, it plunged straight into the cliff face. Here and there scattered on the ground around the great gray rocks were angular white boulders that, even in this dull light, gleamed like beacons. When they came up to them, Vincent stopped and picked one up. It looked something like marble.

"Quartz," said Vincent, who studied geology at school. "Where there's quartz, there's sometimes gold."

"Oh!" said Bobby on a long-drawn-out breath, and the sound was something like the air going out of a tire. He dropped the shovel head. "Then this is only a miner's track, and this is where it's been taking us."

They looked at one another and were silent. Then Vincent said—and his voice had lost its punch—"Well then, we ought to be able to follow it back the other way."

Bobby shook his head. "It stopped in the creek where we found it," he pointed out.

At this point Jane sat down suddenly, put her head on her knees, and made muffled sounds of distress. It was what they all felt like. Vincent sat down beside her. "I can't go any farther," he said.

Bobby stood looking down on them. His mouth looked smaller than ever and his eyes had somehow gone back into his head so that they seemed great shadows in the sockets. It was easy to see the shape of his small, angular skull. "Stay here," he said. "I'm going to have a look at those rocks. There may be somewhere we could spend the night." He turned and trudged off, and his dog followed him.

SEVEN

SANCTUARY

They thought that he was gone a very long time, but they were too weary to do anything but sit there. They did not talk; they did not even think. It was almost as if only their bodies sat there, huddled on the wet ground, and the rest of them, everything that made them Vincent and Jane, had gone away to remote and pleasant tracts of memory. They had watched Bobby, though with very little curiosity, as he stumbled slowly toward the rocks. Then he reached them, turned a corner, and was lost. That was quite a time ago. They had not seen him since. It did not seem to matter whether he turned up again or whether he didn't. They could go on sitting there indefinitely.

But suddenly they heard Bobby's shrill whistle. They looked up. He was standing at the edge of the rocks waving something in his hand and beckoning. If anyone as tired as that could show excitement, Bobby was excited. In a moment they came to life. They did not exactly spring up, but they got up as quickly as they could and made their way toward him. When they got nearer, they saw that he was waving a dead rabbit by the hind legs.

"Skyraider caught it," he said hoarsely. "And there's a beaut of a cave over there. That's where he caught the rabbit. It couldn't get out. We can sleep there tonight. It's dry. And there's wood in it. Come on." His voice was not only hoarse but also quivering. He turned, and they followed him around the rocks. Neither of the others spoke, for it did not seem to be a moment for words.

Once around the corner, they saw that the rocks stretched for quite a distance in a sort of untidy jumble of loose stones of different sizes and great slabs of rock that had at some time shouldered their way up through the earth of the hillside. The stone was sometimes white and sometimes gray, but here and there were gray ones that had been slashed through with streaks of white. Beyond this rough no-man's-land of rock, the slope of the hillside became less precipitous and the gully gave indications of widening out a little.

Bobby worked his way up to where two great slabs of rock rested against one another at an angle, as if they had attempted to form a tent. By doing this, they had held back the slope of the hill so that the earth came down to their peak, and then there was a drop to their base, and the slope continued on from there. On top of them grew an acacia tree, but it had been so stunted and bent by the wind that it had grown horizontally instead of upward and now made a sort of roof over them. Because of the drooping branches of the tree, it was hard to see what lay between the rocks, but Bobby ducked underneath and apparently disappeared into the earth, for he vanished, and then they heard his voice, muffled and echoing strangely, coming from between the rocks. They plunged in after him.

The entrance was smaller than it looked, and Jane and Vincent both bumped their heads on a ledge of rock before they realized they had to bend almost double to get through the opening. Once through, it was possible to stand up straight, and they found that Bobby was standing beside them. Only a little light filtered through the entrance, but when their eyes got used to it, they could just make out the outlines of the cave.

It was quite extensive, although the only place where they could stand upright was where they were now. Toward the back, the roof of rock sloped down and seemed eventually to meet the floor. They could not be quite sure that it did, for the far end was too dark for them to see. The floor was fairly smooth, and where they stood, it was covered with a thickish layer of dry sand. Farther back, it became more uneven as the sand gave place to rock. On the floor against the wall on one side was a jumble of dead leaves, bits of bark and stick. They could have been blown in by the wind, or they could have been left there by some long ago miner. The cave did not look as if it had been used recently and might, indeed, never have been used at all. From somewhere came a draft of surprisingly warm air. This they did not notice at first, but it added unconsciously to their pleasure.

"Oh," said Jane when she could finally find words. "What a lovely little home!"

Vincent collapsed to the floor. "Thank goodness," he

said. "Now we'll be all right for the night." Then he looked curiously at Bobby. "How on earth did you find it? The hole isn't all that easy to see."

Bobby pointed to Skyraider, who was already curled up on a corner of the sand, fast asleep. "He found it," he said. "The rabbit went in here, and he went after it. I could hear him barking as if he was away underground, so I followed."

"Darling Skyraider!" said Jane with great feeling, and then spoiled it by adding, "Even if you are so ugly."

"What are we going to do with that?" asked Vincent, pointing to the rabbit in Bobby's hand. "How can we eat it?"

Bobby fished in his pocket and produced his knife. "I'll skin it with this," he said. "We can make a fire and boil it in the billy. We won't waste so much as if we roast it, and we can drink the water after."

To the three famished travelers it sounded like ambrosia. "We might," said Vincent, and there was a tremor in his voice, "we might even get another." And he looked with new respect at the sleeping Skyraider. In fact, that small, round, quivering black ball with its tan nose tucked under its tail now began to assume an importance in their eyes that it had never had before. Even Bobby regarded his canine hero with new pride.

"Dare say," he said nonchalantly. Then he added, "I'm going outside to skin the rabbit. Who's got the billy?" They had taken turns carrying the billy and had several times been on the point of leaving it behind. They were glad now that Bobby had refused to move without it. Jane held it up.

"You find some water then, Janey," he said. "Have a look around before you go right down to the creek."

Half an hour ago she would have thought it impossible to go down to the creek and back for water. Now she went without a word. The thought of the rabbit—and it was a big one—was making them all swallow at frequent intervals.

Vincent got up and followed Bobby out of the entrance. Bobby turned to him. "You could get as many dryish sticks as possible and then start a fire. We better make it near the door so the smoke'll go out."

Vincent nodded and went off. Bobby was still skinning the rabbit when Vincent came up to him again. "There's enough wood there now to last the night, I think," Vincent said. "None of it's dry, but it's dry enough so it'll burn all right once the fire's started, and we can start it with the wood in the cave."

Bobby nodded. He had his foot on the skin and was engaged, rather gruesomely, in pulling the rabbit out of it by the hind legs. He needed his breath to grunt as he pulled. Seeing that he was too busy to speak, Vincent said in a remarkably humble tone, "Shall I light the fire now?"

Bobby nodded again. It was doubtful whether either of them even noticed that the leadership had changed.

By the time Jane came trudging up the hill with the water, the rabbit was skinned and neatly divided into four pieces.

"Four?" said Jane when she saw it. "But we're only three."

"Skyraider," said Bobby briefly, and she saw that it was just.

They went to the cave together and were gratified to find that clouds of smoke were billowing out of the entrance. They screwed up their eyes, held their breath,

and plunged through. They found a homey scene. Beside
the entrance hole a really healthy little fire was crackling
and sparkling, and beside it, their faces lighted spasmod-
ically by the flickering flames, sat Vincent and Skyraider.
A wisp of steam was rising from Vincent's shoulders.

With great ceremony Bobby placed the pieces of rabbit in the water. Then they put the billy carefully on the
fire, and he sat down with Jane beside Vincent. No one
spoke and no one took his eyes off the billy. They
watched the first little seed-pearl bubbles gather around
the edge, they heard the first high, thin little song of the
heating water, and they sighed when the first whiff of
cooking reached their nostrils. No smell had ever before
charmed them as this one did. Skyraider sat with ears
pricked and nostrils quivering.

The water began to boil, and they leaned forward,
clasping their knees with their arms. It wasn't long before
both Vincent and Jane were inclined to think it was
cooked, and Vincent started to get up.

"Not yet," said Bobby. And Vincent sat down again.

Presently, however, just before what would probably
have been open mutiny, Bobby got up, peered carefully
into the billy, and announced that he thought they could
eat it now. It was removed from the fire. But now they
met with a difficulty. The rabbit stew was far too hot
for them to put their fingers in. They had to wait again.

Eventually the meal was started. The pieces were
handed around, Skyraider politely taking his to a private
corner, where they soon heard him happily crunching
bones. It was plain, unadorned rabbit, but they found it
delicious. When they had finished, they licked their
fingers and took turns drinking from the billy. At the end,

when nothing more remained, Vincent said wistfully, "I wish it had been a calf."

Nevertheless, they were very much revived. For the moment they felt that their troubles, after so long, were over. Even their clothes had begun to dry. Bobby sighed deeply, climbed to his feet, and picked up the billy.

"I'll fill that," he said. "Then we can have a hot drink in the night if we want it." He disappeared out of the hole.

By the time he came back, the fire had been stoked and Vincent and Jane were stretched on the sand behind it. They were almost asleep already. He put the billy down carefully, slid out of his coat, and shuffled himself comfortably on the sand. He yawned.

"It's nearly dark now," he said, "but I think it might be fine tomorrow."

Within five minutes every one of them was asleep. The fire crackled on; Skyraider sneezed, scratched, and curled himself clockwise instead of counterclockwise. Outside, the wind stirred gently and the night deepened.

EIGHT
THE NOISE IN THE NIGHT

It was many hours later when Vincent woke. He was warm and comfortable, and it seemed a pity to move. He was not sure why he had wakened. He closed his eyes. Two minutes later he opened them again. Skyraider had trotted past his head. "Lie down," he hissed, and rolled over. His thoughts were just drifting into fantasy when Skyraider gave a very small whine. Vincent tried to think he hadn't heard it. The whine was repeated a little louder and was accompanied by a faint sound of scratching in the sand. It was no use pretending to himself he was asleep any longer, and he sat up. The fire was very low and the cave was almost dark, but he thought he caught glimpses of a little shadow moving restlessly about at the far, low end of the cave.

"Oh, go to sleep, Skyraider," he said as loud as he dared. There was silence for a minute, and then he heard the sound of scratching again. He got up quietly and put some more wood on the fire. When it flared up, he could see better. It was Skyraider all right, but he was wandering about uneasily, stopping with pricked ears, whining softly, and then trotting a little farther. Often he disappeared altogether into the shadows. Vincent was just telling himself that the dog was probably imagining mice when he heard another sound. This was not Skyraider; it had nothing to do with him; but it made him stop and stand motionless. It was a peculiar noise, something like a very faint and hoarse moan, and the sound of it made a prickling sensation at the back of Vincent's neck. He sat quite still, and his breathing dwindled to nothing. He was halfway through his first deep breath when he heard it again. It seemed to come from the very remotest, darkest part of the cave. He stared into the gloom, feeling that the very strength of his gaze must pierce the blackness somewhere. But all he saw was the deep shadow, the firelight flickering on the rocky roof, and the two silent sleeping bundles beside him. Sitting there staring, he lost count of time and had begun to tell himself it had been imagination or the wind when he heard it again. This time it was more prolonged and a little louder; a wail, deep and desperately sad. When it stopped, the silence rushed back into the cave. He could stand it no longer, and he shook Bobby into waking.

"Listen," he whispered as soon as Bobby opened his eyes. But for a time the sound was not repeated. Their whispering woke Jane, and she, too, sat up.

"What's the matter?" she asked sleepily. She had not attempted to whisper, and her voice sounded suddenly loud in the quiet cave.

"Hush!" they both said, but it was too late, and this time there was no mistaking the long, low moan that came from somewhere behind them. Skyraider gave one loud whimper and suddenly rushed out into the night.

"What was it?" said Jane, and now she was whispering.

"Vincent's been hearing it for quite a time," whispered Bobby. "He doesn't know what it is."

"Do you?" asked Jane in a strained voice.

Bobby shook his head.

"What'll we do?" asked Jane, and funnily enough, both she and Vincent looked at Bobby. But he only shrugged his shoulders.

"Don't know," he said. "I suppose anyone who wanted to could go outside."

Silence greeted this logical suggestion. None of them seemed inclined to move. Then Bobby, who had been looking thoughtfully into the fire, spoke again.

"Have you noticed how nicely the smoke blows out of the door?" he asked.

"So it does," said Vincent, who noticed it now for the first time and was surprised that Bobby should remark on such a detail at a time like this. But then Bobby said, "Sign there's a draft coming from the back somewhere."

They all looked nervously behind them into the recesses of the cave. As if in answer, the moaning started once more, continued for perhaps five seconds, and then died away. They moved closer together, facing the sound, glad of the honest fire at their backs.

"That nice warm air," said Jane after a time. "It must have come from the back of the cave."

Bobby looked at her steadily as if he willed her not to be frightened. "So there's a hole there that we can't see," he said.

"Of course!" said Vincent rather loudly, slapping his knee, and with that they heard the sound again.

"It comes when we talk loudly," said Bobby in a whisper.

"I was going to say it must be the wind," said Vincent, and his whisper quivered the smallest bit. "But I don't think it is."

"No," said Bobby. He got up and put some more wood on the fire and then sat down again. Two things now seemed important, though they could not have said why. One was that the fire should not be allowed to die down; the other was that they must not turn their backs on the interior of the cave.

"Skyraider's gone," said Jane after a long silence. Nobody answered, and she added, "They say a dog always knows."

"Skyraider's a fool," said Bobby, and it was the first time he had ever been disloyal to his dog. But Jane's breathing became a little slower.

Vincent suddenly thought of the billy. They boiled it, had a hot drink, and felt a little better. From time to time the moaning was repeated. It became no less terrifying, but at least it got no louder and came no nearer, and in a way they learned to put up with it. In time they even managed to drop off into an uneasy kind of sleep, for they slept propped against one another, sitting up, and they all dreamed dreams. And Skyraider did not return to the cave that night.

Eventually the night passed. When the first light of morning filtered in through the small round entrance hole and they woke and found themselves still whole, still warm, dry, and unharmed, their spirits rose.

"More hot water," said Bobby. He picked up the billy

and went out. When he came back, the fire was bright, and Vincent and Jane were warming their hands in front of it. They did not even turn around, although they might have shivered a little, when the now familiar moan rose up behind them, cracked into something like a sob, and died away again.

"The sun's coming up," he said, and they could hear the excitement in his voice. "It's going to be fine, I think, and there's a sort of a track farther along down the hill."

"Oh," said Vincent with great satisfaction. "If only the sun stays out, we'll be all right." He was almost his old, robust self.

At that moment there was a snuffle at the entrance, and Skyraider trotted in. He wagged his tail vaguely at them and went straight to the back of the cave, where he spent some time sniffing and scratching.

"Found him down there by the creek somewhere," said Bobby. "Something's got him bothered." Suddenly he sprang to his feet. "I'm going to see," he said, and dragged a piece of blazing bark from the fire.

"No, Bobby," said Jane sharply, and clutched at his coat.

Bobby twitched it away. "Let me alone," he said. "It won't hurt." He approached the far end, bending low as he went and holding the flame in front of him. Vincent said nothing, but he rose to a squatting position in readiness for any quick movement that might be necessary.

As the flame drew nearer to the far corner, they noticed that the draft blew it more and more strongly backward until it threatened to go out altogether. Bobby sheltered it with his hand and crawled forward. He had to bend lower and lower. Somewhere ahead of him they could hear Skyraider snuffling and whimpering. The

madly flickering flame made queer dancing shadows on
the ceiling, and from time to time they thought that
something moved. But Bobby went on, and now it seemed
that he was wriggling on his stomach, for his voice came
to them distant and muffled.

"There's a hole down here all right," he said. "It doesn't
seem to be very big and it's too dark to see, but it goes
down a long way. I'm coming out." He proceeded to
wriggle out backward, and they saw that he was smoth-

ered with cobwebs and dust, like a bottle of old crusted
port. He stood up, sneezed, and rubbed the dust out of
his eyes. "No good," he said. "Where's my hot drink?"

And they found that the billy had been boiling away
unnoticed for some time.

"The noise must have come up that hole," said Bobby
as they drank. "It probably came from miles and miles
away."

With this comforting thought they finished their hot
drink, buttoned up their coats, and climbed out of the
cave. The morning was clear and lovely, and their eyes
were dazzled by the unaccustomed light. But the noise
did not come from miles and miles away, and before
they had gone very far, they found the source of it.

They started off down the hill, for Bobby pointed out the faint marks down by the creek that might once have been a track. They led onward and not back where they had come from, which was what they had expected. And now that the clouds were dispersed, they could see that it led to a milder countryside with wider valleys and lower hills. There was still no sign of a building anywhere, but the sight of several small cleared paddocks lifted their hearts. It was so long since they had seen anything made by men.

As they descended, they found that the lower part of the hillside among the tumbled rocks was full of upturned earth and pockmarked with strange holes. The earth was all overgrown now, and the holes had apparently been filled in again, but there was no doubt that at some time something had done a great deal of burrowing here, and it was no rabbit, either.

"More like grizzly bears," said Vincent.

But Bobby, who had been poking around, said, "I think probably miners." He looked up suddenly. "It was around one of these that Skyraider got so excited. Now which one?" He looked for his dog.

"There," said Jane, pointing to where, a little farther down the hill, Skyraider's tail and hindquarters appeared from behind a rock. They were moving convulsively, jerking up and down and from side to side but not moving from the spot.

"Poor dog's gone mad," said Vincent rather unkindly.

"I think he's only digging," said Bobby. And when they reached him, they found that this was so. Just below one of the bigger of the old mine shafts he was digging frenziedly. Showers of damp earth poured out from between his hind legs, and his nose was covered with mud. He had already made quite a hole.

"No rabbits there, silly," said Jane.

But Bobby suddenly said, "Shsh!" and cocked his head. They listened. And then they heard it, quite loud now—the moan that they had heard in the cave.

"It's inside the mine shaft," said Bobby, and began pulling at the old pieces of corrugated iron and the heavy, rotten old planks that boarded in the hole. In one corner the boards had rotted away completely, and there was an opening perhaps eighteen inches square. It was near this that Skyraider was digging his own hole.

Jane caught Bobby's arm. "Don't, Bobby," she said. "You don't know what's there."

"But I'm going to find out," he said. "Let me go, Janey. Something alive's down there."

And then Vincent, who had been watching him a little strangely, took a breath, came up, and started to help him. Jane, torn between anxiety and curiosity, stood back a little, her eyes very big and fixed on the hole and her knuckles in her mouth.

Bit by bit the covering came away, and the miner's hole revealed itself. It was about four feet in diameter and led straight into the hillside. Bobby crawled in, feeling his way with his hand as he went. Then he backed out suddenly.

"Drops down," he said, "into a sort of hole. Give us the matches." Vincent passed them over, and he crawled in again. This time he disappeared for perhaps ten minutes before he reappeared. His face was red with excitement and the rich, volcanic earth.

"There's a dog at the bottom," he said. "Around the

corner of some rocks. It's hard to see, and it's steep down, but I'm sure it's a dog. That's what we heard."

"But how could we hear it right up there?" said Jane.

"Easy," said Vincent in the tone of one from whose mind a great load has been lifted. "I'd say these rocks are riddled with holes. There could easily be a sort of shaft from here up to our cave. It wouldn't have to be big to let the sound and the air come up. Poor thing, howling all night, and goodness knows how long before we heard it." Vincent was his old self again.

"We've got to get the dog out," said Bobby, looking around him in some perplexity.

"How?" asked Jane. "We haven't got a rope or anything."

"A branch would do," said Bobby. "If it was cornery enough, he could climb up it."

After quite a search, Vincent managed to break off a rather stunted little sapling that was growing among the rocks. It was considered to be cornery enough to be worth a try. Bobby disappeared into the hole once more, propelling the sapling before him, stalk first. They could hear him, after a time, deep in the earth making encouraging noises. For some time it was a sort of patient, monotonous pleading; then they could hear a note of excitement that increased suddenly to a muffled shout, and Bobby's backside shot into view. He scrambled out, dragging after him by the scruff of the neck a large, shaggy brown dog. It was of no perceptibly single breed, yet it must have numbered various kinds of sheep dog in its ancestry. It had an old gray muzzle and wide, kind eyes. But although it had the look of a well-fed dog, it was now very hollow, and it was covered with dust. Also, they noticed later that its forepaws were rubbed raw and its claws were splintered and cracked from digging. It came to the surface, shook itself, blinked in the light for a minute, and then suddenly was overcome with joy at its deliverance. It was very weak, but as far as it was able, it bounded around them squirming and twisting and giving little yelps and whines of joy. As it cavorted about, the children looked at one another, and each of them smiled a wide, satisfied smile.

Skyraider approached with his head up, stepping high, tail aloft and quivering. The dog stood still, panting, and they touched noses. The quiver in Skyraider's tail changed to a gentle wag, and the strange dog continued its joyful bounding. But now it bounded with more purpose, and they saw that it was making for the creek. It reached the bank, lowered its head, and started to drink. It became completely absorbed and stayed there for a long time.

"Poor thing," said Jane. "It must have been terribly thirsty. I wonder how long it's been down in that horrid hole?"

"A few days perhaps," said Vincent. "It couldn't have stayed there much longer without water. Lucky for it we heard it."

"Yes," said Jane, suddenly overcome with noble, if slightly inaccurate, feelings. "And it was worth all the frights it gave us just to be able to save its poor life. I'd willingly go through another night like that if I knew."

Bobby pricked her shining bubble. "Wouldn't be like that if you knew," he pointed out.

But the dog had now finished drinking. It came up from the creek toward them, stopped and looked back up the creek, and then turned to them once more. They were wondering just where to go next when the dog decided for them. It gave a little whimper and trotted toward what Bobby had taken for an old track. It seemed to have no doubt where it wanted to go. After a little distance it stopped and looked back at them.

"Come on," said Bobby. "We'll follow it."

NINE
THE HOUSE IN THE VALLEY

They moved forward, and the dog, seeing that they were following, gave a little bark of satisfaction and continued on its way.

Afterward, they always said that the dog went slowly so that they could keep up. But it was also possible that having sore paws and being tired and hungry may have had something to do with it. Anyway, all that morning they were able to keep it in sight. It never hesitated, seldom stopped, and led them always down from the hills and toward the cleared country they had seen when they first came out of the cave. They followed as fast as they were able, which was not at any very spectacular pace, for by now their feet were hurting, their shoes were stiff and hard, and they were still fairly tired and very hungry.

But they had no doubt now that they were making for somewhere definite, for all the while the country be-

came easier to travel in. They left the rocky outcrops behind, and more and more grass took the place of timber
on the hills. When at last the dog led them straight to a
gate in the first fence they had seen for three days,
they felt that their troubles were over. They forgot about
their feet, their empty stomachs, their weary legs. They
climbed over the gate, for it was padlocked, and stepped
out along the now clearly defined track on the other side.

"Today's the end of our week," said Jane suddenly.
"They'll start looking for us now, just when we've found
ourselves again."

But they had not yet seen their first house, and even
when they did, all their problems were not solved.

They saw the telephone line long before they saw the
house. It crossed a hill almost directly in front of them,
came down to their track, and from then on accompanied
them on their way. It was obviously a homemade line,
for the posts, though adequate, were not evenly matched,
and here and there, where nature had provided a convenient tree, the line was slung to that to save the felling
of one more sapling and the digging of one more post
hole. This was so makeshift that they knew themselves
to be some way still from the nearest center of any kind,
since a paternal Post Master General's Department did
its best to provide communications for even the remoter
townships.

Knowing they were no longer on their own raised their
spirits considerably. They followed the line until they
came to a place where the track crossed a soak in the
hillside. There had apparently been a big tree growing
here, which, at some time quite recently, had failed to
retain its grip any longer in the sodden ground. The wind
of a few nights ago had probably been the last straw,

and it had fallen with head downhill, right across the telephone line, which lay twisted beneath it. There was nothing they could do, and they continued on, realizing that the telephone line that went with them was very probably useless from this point on.

They saw the house about midday according to Vincent's calculations with the sun. They had just emerged from a grove of trees onto a cleared hillside. Below them, they could see another thick belt of trees and, beyond, a cleared valley much broader than any they had seen so far. It was divided by fences here and there, and they could see tracks running across it. On the far side, on the southern slope and facing north, was a weatherboard cottage. Behind it were several sheds and outhouses and a set of sheepyards. And, best of all, out of the chimney came a long, thin column of smoke.

"Saved!" cried Jane, prepared to enjoy a touch of drama now that the worst was over.

The dog continued to lead them down the hill toward the belt of timber at the bottom, and they could see now that the trees concealed a river—it was too wide to be called a creek—that came out from among the hills behind them, wound its way down the side of the valley, its course marked by casuarinas, and disappeared again into a gap in the hills on the far side. At the moment it was in flood and was moving swiftly, well beyond the limit of its banks on either side. The track took them through the trees and ended abruptly at the brink of the water. There was no bridge, and although there was probably a hard bottom, it was now far too deeply submerged to be of any use. They looked upstream and downstream as far as they could see but found no way of crossing.

"Could we swim?" asked Jane. The water did not look inviting.

"I doubt if any of us are strong enough swimmers," said Vincent, who knew his cousins had not been able to swim very often.

"I suppose we could try if we had to," said Bobby. "I'd rather see if there's another way over first."

So they tried upstream. It was not long before the river narrowed where it came out of the hills, and the banks began to rise more steeply from it. They proceeded farther, and soon the river raced and roared furiously through a narrow channel with the foliage of the trees that fringed the edge of either bank almost touching in the middle. Suddenly Vincent, who was leading the way, stopped and pointed into the trees above their heads.

"What's that?" he asked.

They looked and saw that two thin wire ropes crossed the river high up on the level of the trees. They seemed to be attached to a tree trunk on either side.

They found, when they reached the ropes, that they were a practical little arrangement for conveying small things from one side to the other. Attached to one wire rope, and at the moment on their side, was a pulley from which a hook was suspended. The other wire rope ran through it. A windlass with a handle, beside the tree it was attached to, suggested how the pulley might be operated. Vincent turned the handle. There was a squeak, and the pulley jerked and stuck.

"Half a mo'," said Bobby, and unhooked it from its resting place against the tree. "Try now."

Vincent wound again, and this time the pulley ran smoothly out along the wire. He continued to wind, and they watched it move slowly across the river until it came to rest with a slight bump on the other side. Then he wound it back again.

"Neat," said Bobby. He walked over to the drum on which the wire was wound, bent down, and inspected it carefully. They saw him pick up a stick and poke at the wire. Then he went over to the handle and turned until the pulley had slid some distance out over the river. He returned and inspected the drum once more. Something seemed to be bothering him, and the other two watched in silence. After he had fiddled a bit longer he stood up.

"Here, Vince," he said. "Look at this."

Vincent walked over and looked where his finger pointed. One coil of the wire rope that now lay exposed on the drum had had to pass over a bolt on the drum itself and in consequence had become frayed and worn. Only one of the three strands was holding it together.

"Of course there'd still be one wire holding," said Vincent after he had studied it for a few minutes. "It wouldn't *all* carry away."

"No," said Bobby, "but anyone out there'd be pretty uncomfortable, and they couldn't get back unless there was someone on the pulley on the other side. I reckon they must use this only for bread and the mail." He sounded sad as he said it, as if a hope had faded.

"But, Bobby," said Jane with horror. "You weren't thinking *we* might cross on that thing, were you?"

"I just wondered," said Bobby.

"Well, anyway," said Vincent with something of his old heartiness, for he found the thought of civilization, even with a river between, very cheering, "anyway, there must be other places to cross."

"Shouldn't think so," said Bobby. "Else why would they put this thing here?"

By the time they had gone a little farther upstream, they began to think he must be right, for they soon saw that they had no hope of crossing for some distance. The gorge simply got steeper and the country wilder. They felt in no state to tackle the sort of climb that this promised to be, so they turned back.

Bobby looked wistfully at the wire as they passed it again, but he said nothing, and they returned to the place where they had first met the river. There was no doubt, now that they saw it a second time, that this was the usual crossing place. They could see the tracks going up the bank on the far side and winding away through the trees that fringed the river and out on the cleared paddock that lay beyond. It was obviously the track that led to the weatherboard cottage with the smoke coming out of the chimney. But just as obviously, there was no crossing it now. The collection of logs and branches sweeping along in the current made this impossible. Even an automobile would have been bowled over and battered to bits in no time. A man would not stand a chance. They turned wearily downstream.

They had gone a little distance when Vincent suddenly said, "What's happened to the dogs?"

They stopped, looked behind them, peered into the scrub to the left of them, sheltered their eyes from the sun, and looked farther ahead. They stood quite still and listened. But there was no sign at all of the dogs.

"I don't believe we've seen them since we first reached the river," said Jane.

"Funny," said Vincent. "Where could they have got to?"

Bobby said nothing, but when he had satisfied himself that there were no dogs either to be seen or heard, he put two fingers in his mouth, took a deep breath, and blew. The result was earsplitting, but it brought no result. "Expect the noise of the river drowns it," said Bobby. "I'd better do it again."

This time it was even louder, and Jane and Vincent both felt that nothing less than a nuclear explosion could drown such a piercing note. And this time it produced a result. A small black and tan object shot out of the scrub from somewhere down along the riverbank and came at Bobby like a cannonball. One would have thought that Skyraider had not seen his master for a week.

"But where's the other dog?" said Jane.

When, after a few minutes, it failed to turn up, they looked at one another. "Do you think it's died?" asked Jane.

"Surely not now," said Vincent.

They were still wondering when Skyraider left them to trot down to the water's edge. As he barked and wagged his tail, they noticed that he was watching something on the other side.

"There it is," said Bobby. "Look!" He pointed, and they saw that the strange dog was standing at the water's edge, watching them.

"Where did it cross?" asked Vincent.

"Come on," said Bobby quickly. "Let's find out."

They started off once more, and after one last look at them, the dog on the other bank turned and trotted off through the trees. It moved awkwardly, for its feet were very sore.

For a time the banks on both sides of the river were fairly flat and must, in normal times, have been boggy and full of reeds. Now the water covered them and spread, wide and uncompromising, from side to side. The children were making as good a pace as they could, but apparently it was not fast enough for Skyraider, for he raced ahead as if he were on familiar ground. They followed him until the river narrowed once more to wind its way around a spur of the rough country behind. The bank on their side became steeper, and ahead of them a high outcrop of rock pushed its way out into the river, forcing the water to boil and crash its way through a deep, narrow channel between this and some lower rocks on the opposite side. Once through, it widened out once more until, presumably, it reached the hills on the far side of the valley.

Onto this outcrop of rock Skyraider now led them. They followed, because as far as they could tell this was the most likely place for a crossing they had yet seen. But when they came to the point of the rock and looked down at the frothing river below, they began to wonder if Skyraider had made a mistake. The rocks on the other side were certainly not far away, but they were at a much lower level, and every so often an eddy of the river would swish over them, leaving them black and glassy-looking.

"Oh," wailed Jane. "This can't be the place. He's led us wrong. That other dog must have swum after all."

"But its coat wasn't wet," said Bobby. "And I believe we could get over here." He paused and then said, "Look at Skyraider."

Skyraider was trotting backward and forward along the edge of the rock, looking out over the water and giving little whimpers of distress.

"What is he looking for?" asked Vincent.

"Wait," said Bobby. "Watch him."

They waited. Skyraider got more and more excited. He darted about and scrabbled on the rock with his little claws. Suddenly he stood still, leaned forward, tense and trembling, and then, to their surprise, sprang off the rock. They saw his small body sail through the air, clear the froth and turmoil of the river, and land on the rock below. He slipped, scratched frantically with his claws, and scrambled up the rock to safety.

"There," said Bobby. "That's how the other dog got across."

"But *we* can't," said Jane in a high and quavering voice. "I couldn't. I'd fall."

"We've got to," said Bobby. "We can't stay here." He stepped forward and peered over. "It's not as bad as it looks. I think we can."

"If we go," said Vincent suddenly, "we can't get back."

"Do we want to?" said Bobby, and Vincent slowly shook his head.

Bobby turned to Jane. "I'll go first and you come after me. I'll catch you. It'll be all right." He gave her one of his rare and sudden smiles. Some might have thought it strange that someone so small and thin could speak confidently of catching anyone as round and plump as Jane, but just then it did not seem strange to any of them. He handed Vincent the billy.

"Throw it after me, will you, Vince," he said.

He walked toward the edge, hitched up his belt and would have tightened it if it had not been in the last hole already, took a step back, gauged the distance, and flung himself into space. They held their breath as he landed on the rock on all fours. But he scrambled to his feet, turned around, and waved.

"It's easy." His voice floated up over the noise of the water. "Come on, Janey."

Jane gasped and flung a wild look at Vincent.

"Go on," he said. "You can do it. I'll come after you."
Slowly she moved back as far as the rock would allow
and stood, crouched, as if she waited for the starter's
whistle.

Vincent, with a sudden inspiration, shouted, "Go!" She
rushed forward like a small whirlwind, gathered herself,
and jumped. Vincent saw her land on her feet, slip backward, wave her arms wildly to regain her balance—and
then Bobby's hands came around her, clutched at her
clothing, and with a great heave he pulled her up the rock.

When Jane was safely off the slippery rock, Vincent
threw the billy over, wondering if that was the last they
would see of it. But Bobby fielded it successfully and
then stepped back to wait for him. It was not so difficult
for him because he was taller, and he landed successfully
on the rock just before the river came swishing and hiss-
ing over it. They collected themselves, climbed off the
rock, and arrived safely on the dry ground.

"Well," said Vincent, "if there's no other way out of
this valley, we're here to stay."

"Oh, there must be," said Bobby, "surely." They set
off back along the river to pick up the track.

When they reached it and had put the river thankfully
behind them, Vincent said, "All we've got to do now is
to go down to the house, ask for a cup of tea or perhaps
a roast ox, and if they can direct us to the nearest post
office."

"Oh, Vincent," said Jane, giggling at the first mild
witticism he had uttered for some time.

They came out of the trees quite soon and saw the
house not very far away, across a couple of paddocks.
A line of telephone posts crossing the paddocks a little

to their left showed them the property's one link with the outside world.

"And I suppose that's broken now," said Bobby.

They climbed over a fence and crossed the first paddock. It was full of sheep, and Bobby sternly called Skyraider to heel. With the house so near, they had almost forgotten their tiredness, and oddly enough, their hunger seemed to have disappeared, too.

By the time they were in the second paddock, they could see the hedge around the front garden and the washing on the line in the orchard.

"Oh," said Jane, "doesn't it look lovely and homey?"

A big red cow with a small calf mooed at them as they passed. They went through a gate into a yard that contained dog kennels, strolling fowls, and a shed full of farm machinery. They reached the back gate of the garden at the same time that a young woman came out of the orchard carrying an empty clothesbasket. She was small, slight, and dark, with a pale, calm, and almost childlike face. Her hair was cut short and clung close to her head except where it fell, at the moment, over her forehead in a few halfhearted little curls. She wore a blue dress whose color had been mellowed by frequent visits to the washtub.

Her calm expression vanished when she saw the three children at the gate. They saw her eyebrows shoot up in a startled arch over the top of her horn rims.

"Good gracious!" she said, and her voice was pleasant and pitched rather low. "Whatever are you doing here?"

Vincent came forward. He now wore his very best manners, something far in excess of anything Jane or Bobby could produce. "Excuse me," he said, "we're awfully sorry to bother you, but we happen to be lost. We

wondered if you could help us, and perhaps—er"—here he swallowed—"give us something to eat."

Her eyebrows rose, if anything higher than before, and now she looked at them more closely. She saw three tattered, dirty, and extremely disreputable children, whose hair looked as if it had been unacquainted with a brush or comb for many a long day. Her glance also encompassed Skyraider, whose snippy little face never had revealed what Bobby considered to be his true worth. But she saw also that the dark rings around each pair of eyes were not entirely of dirt, that the cheeks were hollow, and that the polite smiles that greeted her were there only by an extreme effort of will, for the wearers were exhausted to the point of collapse.

She wasted no further time in explanations. "Come in, then," she said. "I'll fix you up." She turned and led the way toward the house.

They had walked up the garden in silence and were approaching the back door when Jane suddenly said in a loud and surprised voice, "Oh, *there* he is," and rushed forward, flinging herself on the brown, shaggy dog that rose slowly from the doormat.

The young woman put her hand out quickly and made a sharp exclamation but, seeing that the meeting was indeed a pleasant mutual surprise, let it fall again. The dog's tail wagged, and Jane's plump arms clasped its neck. Skyraider stood stiffly beside them, his tail, also, vibrating a greeting.

"You seem to know Priscilla," said the young woman, perhaps a trifle unnecessarily. "I was going to tell you to be careful because she's shy of strangers. She sees so few."

"We're not exactly strangers—" began Vincent, but Jane interrupted him.

"It—Priscilla—brought us here," said Jane. "She showed us the way and how to cross the river and everything."

The young woman looked exceedingly puzzled. "I wondered where she'd been," she said slowly. "I've been so worried about her. I hunted everywhere. I thought she might have been caught in a fence. But she came back this morning by herself. Something must have happened to her because she was starving and her front paws are sore. Where did you come across her?"

"As a matter of fact," said Vincent, taking the matter into his own hands, "we found her this morning down a mine shaft. She might have been there for ages. And she sort of led us back here and then left us when she saw us go to the crossing place. We didn't know where to go, you see." He looked at her as if all was now perfectly plain.

She still looked puzzled and would have liked to know more, but she pulled herself up. Bobby, she saw, was swaying on his feet. This was no time for explanations. She opened the door.

"Well, never mind now," she said. "Later on you must tell me a lot more. But I think we'll just get you fed and into bed for the moment." They followed her in.

She did ask them then one or two more questions, but these dealt solely with when they had last eaten and how much and when they had had their last good meal. Their answers were confusing, but she gathered enough to realize that they must all be exceedingly hungry. She gave them each a small bowl of bread and milk.

"I know you don't think it's enough," she said. "But if you've only had one rabbit between you—"

"And Skyraider," said Bobby.

"And Skyraider, of course, then I can't give you a great big meal or you'll all be sick. And so will Skyraider. You must have that and then a sleep, and then you shall have some more."

So they ate their bread and milk, and although they had long ago ceased to feel hungry, it seemed to them the most magnificent meal they had ever had. And afterward they were rolled onto beds and covered with blankets. But by that time they scarcely knew what was happening to them. Only Bobby made a mental note of the fact that the young woman had fed them and put them to bed and pulled their shoes off and had not so far once asked them to wash. He sighed deeply and contentedly, feeling that they had fallen into good hands.

TEN
LET THE POLICE KNOW

That night ended the week that they had been allowed, and while they slept their first real sleep for three nights, Mr. and Mrs. Thompson sat in their armchairs on either side of the sitting-room fire at Rosedale and looked at one another. At least, Mrs. Thompson looked at Mr. Thompson. He alternately looked at her, read the paper, leaped up and snatched his pipe from the mantelpiece, lit it, took a few puffs and knocked it out, read the paper again, and once more looked at her.

"Of course they may not have started till dusk," said Mrs. Thompson in a terribly cheerful voice.

Mr. Thompson did not reply, so she said, "And it would take them quite a time to ride home in the dark. Especially if they didn't tie the pack on very well and it kept falling off."

Mr. Thompson nodded, grunted, and refilled his pipe.

"Their horses could easily have gotten out of the pad-dock," continued Mrs. Thompson hopefully. "And it would take them hours to catch them in that big paddock —especially in the dark." There was a pause, and then she added in a voice from which the brightness had faded, "Wouldn't it?"

Mr. Thompson sprang up. "It's ten o'clock," he said. "And they ought to be home. A hundred and one things *may* have happened to them. But they ought to be home." He slapped the table with the palm of his hand and then strode over to the window and flung the curtain back. He might have been looking into a pool of ink for all he saw. With a grunt of disgust he turned away.

"All I can say is they'll be sorry when they do come back," he exclaimed with great ferocity.

For a time there was silence, and then Mrs. Thompson said, "I keep wondering how I had best break it to Helen. One can't very well say, 'We have lost your son.' It's going to be very awkward."

"For goodness' sake, Frances!" said Mr. Thompson, who, like most parents became extremely cross when he was anxious. "Try to see the thing reasonably. You can't call them lost when we know where they are. If they don't turn up, all I've got to do is to go and get them."

Mrs. Thompson cleared her throat. "Well, wouldn't you—that is, when would you reasonably consider we could definitely say they hadn't turned up? I mean, they haven't, have they?" she ended in a burst of despera-tion.

"Well, you can hardly expect me to turn out in the middle of the night, can you?" said Mr. Thompson.

As this was exactly what Mrs. Thompson did expect, she wisely said nothing.

"After all, if I found them halfway home, as I almost certainly should, I'd look a pretty sort of fool, wouldn't I?" He glared at his wife.

This, she realized, was the crux of the matter, and she plunged. "Not at all, dear," she said with great conviction. "If they're still coming home at this hour, I should think they'd be *immensely* relieved to see you."

Mr. Thompson gave a snort. "If they're coming home at this hour," he said, "and they're so particularly anxious to see me, I'll wait here under the light." And with that he picked up his paper once more and appeared immediately to become deeply engrossed in its contents.

Mrs. Thompson stifled a sigh and started some neglected darning.

The night wore on, and Mr. Thompson was steadfast in his refusal to take any action until next day. At midnight they put out the light and went to bed. As they left the sitting room, he said, "I'll just slip out and make sure I tied up the dogs." And Mrs. Thompson, knowing quite well that he never failed to tie up his dogs when he fed them, nodded casually, as if it was his nightly practice.

To Mrs. Thompson, at any rate, it was a very long night. Twice she got up and went out onto the veranda, thinking she heard a noise; twice she returned to bed, pulled up the bedclothes, and told herself that worrying was a waste of time. But she knew when the first cock crew, when the first little dawn wind lightly stirred the curtain, and when the trees outside the window first put on substance and became distinguishable from the surrounding shadows. Mr. Thompson lay quietly and even snored from time to time. But the sun had not yet risen when he threw back his bedclothes, sat up, yawned, stretched, and announced that he thought he'd get up. It was an hour and a half before his accustomed time.

"After all," he said, as if they had been discussing it all night, "the chances are they were held up by the bad weather and didn't manage to finish on time."

They had their breakfast quickly, and while Mrs. Thompson washed up, he went to fetch the Landrover from the shed. She was ready for him by the time he'd filled its tank with gasoline and brought it around to the house. She had the first-aid kit in her hand and was trying to conceal it behind the cardigan she also carried. But he saw it.

"What on earth makes you think you'll need that thing?" he demanded. "Just because they don't turn up on time doesn't necessarily mean they're all badly injured."

Mrs. Thompson looked guilty. "I know," she said. "It's just that I feel so much happier when I have it." She gave him her very sweetest smile as she got in, banged the corner of the case against his knee, and then laid it carefully on the floor beneath her feet. "Silly of me, isn't it?" she said.

The sun was still throwing long shadows across the grass as they set out over the paddocks in the direction the children had traveled exactly one week before. After the rain it was such a clear and sparkling morning that it seemed impossible they should not find the children safe and well when they reached the boundary rider's hut. After about half an hour's traveling, when the wheel track began to peter out on the stony hillsides, Mr. Thompson said that there was no point in knocking the guts out of the thing by driving any farther, and he would walk the rest of the way.

"You can wait here," he said as he got out.

But Mrs. Thompson had had enough of waiting, and she got out too, lifting the first-aid kit out afterward.

"You're not carrying that all the way, are you?" he said.

"No point in bringing it all this way if we don't have it when we need it," Mrs. Thompson replied with a cheerfulness that was not altogether convincing. "I can carry it; it's not heavy."

Mr. Thompson said nothing but pressed his lips rather tightly together and took it out of her hand. They started up the hill in silence.

When the boundary rider's hut came into view, they stopped. Mr. Thompson pointed. "There," he said, "you see. There are the ponies. Perfectly all right and not even saddled up yet. They're probably all still asleep."

Mrs. Thompson looked at the small hut, from which came no sign of life, and then at the four horses, placidly cropping grass down by the creek. Her face became pink.

"Well, really!" she said crossly. "That *is* the limit! I shall go straight down and give them a piece of my mind." And like an avenging fury she set off with great strides down the hill.

Mr. Thompson followed more slowly. When he reached her, she was standing in the doorway of the hut, her hand to her mouth. "Richard," she said in a kind of whisper, "they're not here."

It was perhaps a quarter of an hour later when Mr. Thompson returned to where his wife was sitting on the edge of the veranda. He came with a purposeful step and spoke briskly.

"There's no sign of them anywhere about," he said. "I've been as far afield as I think is practicable at the moment. We'll go home now and let the police know. The sooner something gets moving, the better."

Mrs. Thompson said nothing but followed him quickly up the hill to the Landrover, the first-aid kit in her hand.

ELEVEN
MARY AND CHRISTOBEL

Late that same afternoon Bobby stirred and rolled over. His eyelids fluttered and then lifted. Slowly his memory started to work again, and he remembered where he was and how he had gotten there. A motionless form on a camp bed beside his own he thought he recognized as Vincent. He slipped quietly off the bed and padded out into a narrow passage of polished linoleum, which led him to a moderately large room containing three easy chairs, a table with upright chairs, a large bookcase, and a side table supporting a kerosene lamp. The lamp was already lighted, and the young woman was sitting in the chair beneath it with a baby in her lap. She was trying to feed it with a spoon, and it was crying and did not seem to be cooperating very well. Bobby sidled into the room.

After watching for a minute he remarked, "Not hungry, is he?"

The young woman gave a start and looked around. Then she laughed.

"So you've wakened at last!" she said, and Bobby came a few steps closer. He was pleased to see that the baby was not brand-new but had hair and an intelligent look in its eye.

He said politely, "He seems to be a good sort of a baby."

The young woman nodded. "It's a girl, as a matter of fact. But I'm not sure she's quite well today."

"Touch of colic, I expect," said Bobby. "I say, what's your name?"

She smiled at him. "I've been wanting to ask you that. There are so many things I have been wanting to ask you, but none of you would wake up. Do you know it's twenty-four hours since you went to bed?"

Bobby looked at her in astonishment. At last he said, "Then it must be just about the end of tomorrow by now."

The young woman laughed—a satisfactory sound. In spite of his accustomed gravity, Bobby smiled.

She said, "Yes, I suppose it must be. It makes it awfully complicated, doesn't it? My name's Mary Taylor, and this is Christobel. We call her Chris for short. Now tell me what your name is and how on earth you managed to turn up at my back gate."

Before Bobby could speak, a sound in the doorway made them turn their heads. Jane stood there, tousled, sleepy, and remarkably dirty. "I woke up," she announced, "and I may have wakened Vincent. I fell out of bed."

"Were you hurt?" asked Mary in some alarm.

But Bobby muttered unsympathetically, "About time."

Jane shook her head and came toward them. "No. I just couldn't seem to remember where I was supposed to be. When I came in off that veranda, I couldn't see because of the dark, so I fell over that camp bed that seemed to have Vincent in it. He made a sort of noise when I fell on top of him, so I dare say he is awake."

"It's pretty hard to stay asleep when something the size of Jane lands on top of you," said a voice from the door, and Vincent came into the room.

"Well, never mind," said Mary Taylor. "It's probably time you all woke up and had something else to eat—and a bath," she added as an afterthought. "Tell me all about it while I finish feeding Chris. And then we must think what we're going to do with you. I'm sure I ought to let somebody know." She frowned for a moment and then said, "Now go on."

So they sat on the floor around her and took turns telling her what had happened. Their adventure sounded good as they told it. The part about the moaning in the cave was particularly dramatic, and she exclaimed with horror at the part where Bobby took the burning bark and went to the back of the cave.

"And what could it have been?" she asked breathlessly.

"Priscilla," said Bobby, whose ear for dramatic effect was not quite as keen as his sister's or cousin's.

"So that's where she was!" said Mary. "Poor Priscilla!"

At the end of the story she appeared quite speechless. Finally she said, "I think you all did wonderfully well. What a horrifying experience and how splendidly you all managed! As for finding Priscilla, I can't thank you

enough. She disappeared just after Jack left to see about
the cattle. Jack's my husband. And I didn't know whether
she'd gone with him or what. How could I possibly have
found her? She'd have died." After the trials of the last
three days her praise fell like water on parched ground.
But Christobel suddenly protested loudly, and she sprang
up. "I'll put Chris to bed and try her with this stuff
again later. She's probably just a bit out of sorts. I must
get you children something else to eat." She stood up,
looked them all up and down, and then continued, "On
second thought, I believe I'll light the chip heater. I didn't
want to bother you before when you were so tired, but
I'm sure you'll feel even better when you're clean." She
said it so nicely that it was impossible to object, and now
that their attention was called to how they looked, each
of them could see that the other two would be considerably improved by a bath.

An hour later they all had dinner at the round table.
Their clothes were in the washtub, and they wore pajamas of assorted sizes and colors, rolled up at the knees
and elbows. They shone with cleanliness. But as she put
their plates in front of them, Mary said, "I haven't given
you a great deal because you must still be careful. But
little by little you shall eat more and more."

She sat down and smiled at her oddly clad guests.
"And you mustn't think you're the only ones," she added.
"I have two more patients outside who are being treated
in exactly the same way." They looked puzzled, and she
explained, "I mean Priscilla and your own little dog. They
were both pretty hungry, too, you know. I couldn't get
your dog to settle down till I brought him in and showed
him where you were."

While they ate, she told them how she and Jack came

to be farming in such an unpromising and inaccessible place. It appeared that at first they had searched all over the state for a property they could afford to buy, which was big enough to support them and showed some promise of development. But land prices were high, and they had come to the conclusion that their choice lay between a big piece of poor country out west, which with its chancy rainfall would have been too big a gamble for their slender purse, or a smaller piece of this underdeveloped, rough country in the center of the state, which could offer them a reliable rainfall and a good climate but much hard work.

They had chosen this, feeling that poor soil can be improved, particularly when they were in a position to pay for having it fertilized by air, and that sooner or later the land would become more valuable and easier to manage as properly surfaced roads and electricity were brought closer. In the meantime, they put up with the inconveniences of having to cut their own road through the hills and of providing their own water, light, and heat, and they were only grateful that the mailman had agreed to come out to their mailbox on the other side of the river as often as once a week. As he also brought the bread, groceries, and railway parcels as well, they felt that they were singularly fortunate. They had had, of course, to bring their own telephone line from the nearest point of the line on the main road some twenty miles away.

When they asked where Jack was, she told them that he had had to go away the week before to bring home some cattle they had on "agistment." This meant that they had paid for someone else to keep and feed the cattle for a period when they could not do so themselves. As Jane and Bobby knew, it was a common practice.

"And did he leave you here all by yourself?" asked Jane.

"Well, yes," said Mary, "but neither of us thought I'd be cut off as I am at the moment. I could still get the car over the river when he left, and the telephone wasn't out of order. Now the river has come up since the rain, and I don't know what's happened to the phone. I can't raise the exchange."

The children exchanged glances. Vincent said, "I'm afraid there's a tree across it on the other side of the river. It was far too heavy for us to lift, or we would have."

"Oh, is that what it is," said Mary. "Well, we can't do anything about that. The question is what are we going to do about you? We ought to let someone know. Your parents must be very worried. That reminds me—" She stopped and looked at her watch. "We might just be in time to hear something." She sprang up and switched on the radio. "Let's hope the batteries haven't gone flat."

The announcer's voice came through in a confidential whisper and rose to a shout. Mary lowered the volume as the voice announced, "—still scouring the rough country to the south. Further volunteers are called for and are asked to contact the police station at Tarleton." He went on to announce the hundredth birthday of a Parkes resident, and Mary switched off. The children looked at one another.

"Tarleton's our town," said Jane.

"The police station!" said Bobby hoarsely. "What would they want the police for? It can't be us."

"Silly, they always get the police to hunt for people,"

said Vincent. "It doesn't mean we've done anything wrong, does it, Mary?"

"No, but it does mean they are really worried about you. After all, three days is a long time to be in the scrub. I wish there were some way of letting them know."

They all looked rather solemn. They found it a sobering thought that they had become so important that the police and numbers of other people as well had had to stop their own affairs and look for them. Perhaps they remembered it had not been in the course of duty that they had gotten lost.

"Oh, why did we ever go looking for that horrid waterfall?" said Jane suddenly, and burst into tears.

After a while, when she had been persuaded to have some more pudding and was feeling a little cheered in consequence, they began to discuss the situation.

"The river's too deep for the car," said Mary. "It would stall in the middle, and then we'd be stuck."

"And we can't go back the way we came over," said Vincent. "We just couldn't jump up."

"That wire thing," said Bobby thoughtfully. "I wonder if we could fix it."

"You mean the flying fox?" asked Mary. "I didn't know you'd seen it. But that's only for parcels. It would never carry people."

"And it's broken anyway," said Vincent.

"Broken? It was all right when I used it last. That was only yesterday, when—" She broke off suddenly and looked up.

Bobby looked up, too, his eyes wide. "The mailman!" he said hoarsely.

"Of course!" said Mary. "Why didn't we think of him before?"

They all sighed, and their set faces relaxed. But then Bobby said, "When will he come again?"

Mary put her hand to her mouth. "Not for a week," she said in a whisper. "He comes only once a week."

"It's too long," said Vincent. "They'll have the army out by then."

"Never mind," said Mary quickly, as Jane threatened to dissolve again. "We'll think of something else, and we can always tell him as a last resort."

But it was a long time before they could think of anything that had even the slightest chance of being practical. Vincent suggested rolling logs down and making some sort of bridge, but Bobby reminded him of the very substantial logs they had seen floating down the river as if they had been matches. Jane suggested throwing a rope across and lassoing a branch on the other side, and for a moment she and Bobby looked hopefully at Vincent, feeling obscurely that this was something a scout might be expected to excel at. But Vincent was saved embarrassment when Mary said apologetically that she did not think she could find a rope long enough. Bobby still chewed over the possibilities of the flying fox, wondering if the wire could be mended and if he could get across to do it. But Mary would not hear of their attempting it. For the first time she used her position as a grownup. "It just wouldn't be safe," she said. "And I couldn't allow you to try. I'm sorry."

They went to bed that night with the problem still unsolved.

TWELVE
HORSE AND DRAY

The next morning all the children felt very much better.
Vincent went off with the ax to cut wood for the day,
and Bobby took the milk bucket and went to tackle the
cow.

Although the sky was blue and the sun shone, there
was a warm, heavy stillness in the air that felt unseasona-
ble. The rays of sunshine themselves burned as if they
had passed through a magnifying glass, and the feeling of
the morning was uncertain and a little menacing. Swinging his bucket beside him, Bobby paused on his way to
the cow bail and looked about him. The little valley was
peaceful enough, but with bees and other insects droning
about and the limp appearance of the leaves in the vege-
table garden, it had more the feeling of a summer afternoon. He glanced at the western horizon and was not

surprised to see a few little white clouds climbing vertically into the sky. Whatever efforts they made to cross the river ought to be made soon—this morning if possible. A storm, even if farther off in the hills, could bring the river down harder than ever.

The cow was waiting for him in the bail, and he spoke to her quietly, filling her box with chaff from the bin alongside and fastening the pole into place behind her horns. She rolled her eyes a little and mooed once in faint protest at a stranger. Fortunately, Bobby had been helping with the milking at home recently, or his wrists and forearms would have gotten tired long before the cow was dry. From farther off he could hear Vincent chopping the wood. He began thinking again how they might cross the river. No solution occurred to him until he had finished milking and was walking back to the house. Then he noticed an old tipdray standing under a tree in the yard. It was not considered valuable enough to take up space in the machinery shed. But it still looked strong enough and solidly made. He wondered if there was a horse anywhere in the valley to go with it. He did not remember seeing one.

A little later when they were all sitting at breakfast, he said, "Would you happen to have any horses here?"

"Yes," said Mary, holding the teapot poised over a cup. "There's Jack's horse and a big draft horse we took over with the property. He's somewhere about, though I don't believe we've ever used him. Why?"

"I wondered if that dray you've got out there might get across the river," said Bobby.

"Wouldn't the horse get swept away?" asked Vincent.

Bobby wrinkled his forehead. "I thought the dray

might kind of hold him firm. You know, like an anchor, sort of."

"But supposing it didn't?" said Jane in some alarm. "What then? And us all on the dray?"

"Might have to swim," said Bobby.

"It does sound rather dangerous," said Mary. "Besides, I don't know how the horse would behave."

"We could catch the horse and put him in the dray and find out," suggested Bobby.

"I suppose we could," said Vincent doubtfully.

At that moment Mary looked at her watch and said, "The news!" She got up and turned on the radio. The local news was just beginning, and they found that they had now been moved to first place. After a few preliminaries the announcer said, "The three children who have been missing from their home at Rosedale station near Tarleton have still not been found. Police have found no trace of them and are reported to be considering calling in the services of a tracker. Mr. Thompson, father of two of the children, has asked that no expense should be spared in an effort to locate his son and daughter and his nephew." Then followed the request for more volunteers that they had heard the night before.

"Oh," wailed Jane, "I know he can't afford it." And she dissolved into sobs.

"We'd better try the dray," said Bobby, and this time they all agreed with him.

After breakfast the two boys went off to catch the draft horse, which was in one of the paddocks farther up the valley.

The morning was now, if anything, hotter, and in the windless, heavy air they could hear the river, hidden beneath the distant casuarinas, still roaring its way down from the hills. In the west the cloud bank was just a little higher, and Bobby drew Vincent's attention to it.

"Good thing we're trying today and not leaving it till tomorrow," was Vincent's reply.

The house and its surrounding sheds was, they found, at the south end of the valley, and it was across this end that the river ran. Their way now took them through a narrow strip of ground around the foot of a few scrubby hills that jutted out into the valley as if they had strayed somehow from the main rough range behind. It gave the valley a sort of elbow, so that it was shaped like a bent arm. Once around the corner, they saw that the valley widened out and penetrated some considerable distance into the hills. In contrast to the dark gray-green of the surrounding scrub, it looked brilliant in its new autumn flush of growth. A few head of cattle grazed peacefully, and little groups of sheep were already huddled in the shade under a few big white-box trees that scattered the valley floor. A subsidiary stream apparently came down from the higher country beyond, for an undulating line of basket willows wound its way along at the foot of the hills to the right.

They crossed two fences that bisected the flat and made their way to the line of willows, where they found the horse immediately. He was dozing peacefully in the shade, his head hanging, his tail swishing lazily. He turned out to be a big, heavy-boned bay with great feathered feet and a mass of tangled black mane. He threw up his head when he heard them come, and they saw that he had a patriarchal bristle of fawn whiskers along his bottom jawbone. They caught him without difficulty and led him home.

Mary and Jane came out to meet them. "A bit hairy, isn't he?" said Jane.

"So was Samson," said Vincent, and brought a little giggle from her.

They found the harness at the back of the machinery shed, and Vincent lifted the big collar and hames down from the wall. Everything was thick with dust, but fortunately the rats had left it all alone.

The horse gave a sudden snort as Vincent lifted the collar around his neck, but apart from that, he behaved reasonably well, considering the length of time it must have been since he was last harnessed. He tucked his tail between his legs and jumped forward when he felt the breeching, took a few extra steps when the chain rattled, and rolled his eyes behind the winkers once or twice. Bobby led him over to the dray.

"We'd better be ready to go when he's harnessed up," he said. "He mightn't like standing too much."

"Then I must give you your directions quickly," said Mary. She thought for a moment and then said, "I think you'd better follow the track all the way in. There's a quicker way, but we can't risk your getting lost again, and if you keep to the track, you can go all the way in the dray. It may not be easy to see after all this rain, but keep near the telephone line." She paused and then went on. "You'd better leave the horse and dray with the storekeeper when you get there. Tell him Jack will pick them up later. He knows us and he won't mind. I'd come with you if I could, but there's Chris, and as a matter of fact, I don't think she's very well today."

"We'll be quite all right," said Vincent, "especially after all your lovely food. It was *very* good of you to have us," he finished in a burst of good manners.

"Good-by then," said Bobby. "And thanks—if we get across," he added.

"Oh, Mary, good-by," said Jane. "It's been lovely staying with you, even if we did sleep all the time."

Bobby backed the horse between the shafts, and while Jane held his head, he and Vincent lifted the shafts, slipped them on, and hitched the horse in. Cautiously they hooked up the traces.

"Now," he said, "hop in while I hold his head. Vince, you take the reins."

Vincent and Jane went around to the side and quickly scrambled up. Gingerly Bobby let go of the horse's head and stepped back. The horse continued to stand as if distant memories of other, more hard-working days were filtering back. Bobby whistled softly, and Skyraider came running from behind the shed. He picked him up and threw him into the cart. Then he climbed up himself and took the reins, which Vincent, with rather a relieved look, handed over to him.

"Hang on," said Bobby, and stood with his legs apart and a little bent. He flapped the reins gently on the horse's back and made little encouraging noises. The horse jumped forward and stood still. Then, after a moment's thought he took a few more quick steps. The dray rattled along behind him, its occupants clinging nervously to the sides. Bobby was still on his feet.

"Go on," said Bobby.

The horse took him at his word and suddenly charged forward out of the yard and into the paddock, the dray bounding and plunging behind him. Jane grabbed Skyraider by the scruff of the neck as he slithered about on the floor and pulled him to her. She and Vincent hung on, their legs braced against the sides of the dray, their hands

gripping whatever offered a firm hold. Bobby leaned back against the reins, giving at the knees with every jolt and pulling as hard as he could. For a time they proceeded at a sort of gallop, the great feet pounding, mane flying, and the powerful bay back heaving and rolling like the waves of the sea. If they could have looked behind, they would have seen Mary with her fists clutched against her cheeks and her eyes enormous. Then she flew for Chris and made for the riverbank.

Fortunately, the paddock was flat and fairly large, and Bobby managed to steer their flying chariot in a circle until the gallop changed to a canter and the canter to a trot. He turned the horse's head in the direction of the river. The bay was now in a lather, and his nostrils flared.

"Silly thing," said Bobby between gasps, "wearing himself out."

It was a much more sedate equipage that arrived at the river's bank. But the river was still wide and turbulent.

They drove along to the crossing, turned on to the track, and reached the water's brink. Here the horse stopped.

"Go on," said Bobby, touching his back with the reins.

The horse took a step forward, put his nose to the water, and snorted.

"He thinks it's too deep," said Jane. Vincent said nothing but looked at the strong, bubbling current in front of them. It seemed a long way to the other bank.

Bobby slapped the reins down a little harder and in a sterner voice urged the horse forward. Obediently, the bay took a few steps, and the brown flood swirled around his thick, feathered fetlocks. Gingerly he stepped farther in, ears pricked, neck muscles taut. Now the wheels were in the water, and they had officially left the bank. They were glad the dray stood so high; it gave them some sense of security. Little by little the horse drew them farther in, and little by little the river deepened. It came to his knees, climbed up his legs, lapped at his belly, and the wheels turned slowly along behind him. They could feel the current pulling him, and they could see his big muscles pulling and straining against it. The water was up to the axle now, and the whole heavy vehicle trembled in the current. They were almost halfway and the opposite bank was coming closer every moment when disaster overtook them. The horse had battled bravely, and if he had maintained his steady, dogged pace, he might have succeeded. But he put his foot in a hole, went down, felt the pull of the water threatening to overbalance him, and panicked. Desperately he plunged for the other side. They heard his snort, saw his shoulders, sleek and dripping, heave out of the water—and they felt the dray slip.

"Hang on to the left-hand side," yelled Bobby suddenly, as he squatted on the floor of the dray, wrenching at the reins.

They flung themselves over and, as they did so, felt the wheel touch the bottom again. But the horse plunged again. Both wheels slipped as the dray swung around. They could feel the left-hand wheel trying to lift again and did their best to keep it firm on the river bed. But their combined strength counted for nothing against the surge of water that poured down upon them, and gradually the dray swung down the river, tipping as it went. The horse, feeling himself pulled backward and wrenched almost off his feet, went crazy in the shafts. They swung back toward the bank they had left but farther downstream, where the bough of a casuarina leaned dangerously close, low over the water.

"Grab it!" shouted Bobby. "Grab it!" As he shouted, he was pulling the pocket knife feverishly from his pocket, trying to open the blade with one hand, while the other held the now wet and slippery reins. Vincent prized Jane's hands from the side of the dray, twisted her to face the approaching branch, and shouted, "Now jump!" as it swept over them.

They jumped together, clutching at the branch as it brushed past their faces. Vincent grabbed and hung on, but Jane, after clutching desperately for a few seconds, gave a shriek and slipped with a splash into the river.

Bobby did not see. As they jumped, taking their weight from the upstream side of the dray, the wheel left the bottom, the floor of the dray began to slope, and the whole vehicle began to roll over. Bobby let go the reins, climbed to the edge of the dray, and jumped for the horse's back. As he did so, a little black and tan ball sprang with a yelp of fear from the dray into the river. But nobody saw it.

Clutching at the harness, trying to keep his legs from getting jammed between the horse and the shafts, Bobby worked his way up the heaving, desperate back. Once on the withers, he leaned forward and sawed with his pocket knife at the hame strap. It was old and hard and difficult to cut. The horse was down in the water now, trying not to let himself be pulled sideways by the twisting shafts. Every so often his head went under. The water was swirling around Bobby's waist. He clenched his teeth and went on sawing, holding on by the mane with his other hand. Suddenly there was a twang; the hames fell apart and were immediately dragged off and back by the weight of the traces. The horse leaped forward with a grunt, and Bobby heard the harness tearing as he pulled himself free of the dray. Bobby clung on for dear life. It was the roughest ride he had ever had. Snorting, gasping, plunging, the horse made his way to the bank they had left. As he staggered into shallower water, the dray finally rolled over; its wheels, dripping and still turning, came to the surface; it rolled over again and disappeared down the river.

The horse stumbled out up the bank, and Bobby slipped off. For a few minutes his knees refused to hold him and he had to sit down. But his eyes roved up and down the river in search of Jane and Vincent. At last he saw them. His legs recovered their strength, and he got up and made for the bank.

Mary had reached the river and was now crouched by its edge, one hand grasping the branch of a tree behind her, the other holding a long stick out over the water. The other end of the stick was held by Jane, whose dripping head and shoulders rose dankly from the river. Vincent was half in, half out, trying to reach her before the stick broke in two. Bobby tried his hardest to run toward them, but it was more of a totter than a run. By the time he got there, Vincent had reached Jane and was pulling her to the bank. Mary sat down suddenly as the weight came off the stick. Jane climbed, dripping and wild-eyed, to dry land. They looked at one another, counting heads. Mary was the first to speak.

"I don't think you'd better try to cross the river any more," she said shakily.

A sudden noise behind them, shrill above the noise of the river, made them turn. Mary got to her feet.

"That's Chris," she said. "I suppose she's furious. I had to put her down just anywhere when I saw Jane dive into the river."

Bobby caught the horse, which still trembled but seemed glad of the company, and they made their way home in silence, all the children squelching in their shoes as they walked. As if warning them that attempts to escape would always be severely dealt with, a peal of thunder crashed over their heads and went echoing away over the hills. They looked up and saw that black clouds covered the sky.

The horse was unharnessed, consoled with a handful of oats, and let go. Except for a still rather nervous demeanor, it appeared none the worse for its adventure.

"Well, thank goodness you're all safe," said Mary as they reached the house. "And now we'll have to wait as patiently as we can for the mailman. You mustn't try to cross that river again."

THIRTEEN
OVER THE FLYING FOX

Bobby did not miss Skyraider until dusk, when he went outside to feed him. His whistling brought no response, and he remembered that the last time he could recall having Skyraider with him was crossing the river in the dray. Quickly feeding Priscilla, he put his head in at the back door and called out that he'd be back in a minute. Then, tired as he was, he raced down to the river. It was almost too dark to see, and the rumbling storm clouds overhead made it darker. But every so often a dazzling flash of blue lightning made everything as bright as day. Down by the river under the witchlike trees was not a very nice place to be at such a time. Bobby went up and down calling and whistling, and whenever a flash made it possible, he peered across the leaden sheet of water, trying to see if anything moved on the opposite bank. But it was almost impossible in that brief moment to distinguish rocks from stumps, stumps from tussocks, and tussocks from little black bodies that might have been washed up by the water. As he hunted and struggled over the same pieces of ground over and over again, the rain began to fall. Starting with a few tremendous drops, it increased quickly until, in a few minutes it came down —a black, roaring flood from heaven to mingle with the flood below. It was hopeless to search any longer. Bobby turned and ran for home.

When he reached the house, he told the others that Skyraider was lost, and a sudden quiet fell on them. They all remembered seeing him in the dray, but no one remembered what had become of him. It was not a happy party that sat down to supper that night. They were tired; they had failed to cross the river, broken up the dray, and lost their dog—and Chris gave every appearance of sickening with something. Even Mary felt unequal to putting on a cheerful front. When supper was over, she looked around at the three gloomy faces and said, "We'll just listen once more to the news, and then we shall all go to bed."

She switched on the radio. The search still headed the news. "The two Thompson children and their cousin," said the announcer, "who have been missing from their home for two days have still not been found. Hopes were raised yesterday when the remains of a campfire were discovered in a remote valley in the Abercrombie ranges" —the children exchanged glances—"but they have now faded once more as no further trace of the three has been discovered. If the weather is suitable, aircraft will be used tomorrow to assist in the search."

For a minute no one spoke. Then Bobby said, "Gee!" Then they went to bed.

Much later in the night Jane woke up to hear Chris crying in a peevish, tired voice. She heard Mary get up and go into the kitchen. She waited a minute and then climbed out of bed, tiptoed through the room where the boys were sleeping, and felt her way down the passage. Mary was bending over the lamp at the kitchen table, trying to light it. Hearing a sound at the door, she looked up.

"Oh, Jane," she said, "did Chris wake you? I'm so sorry."

"It doesn't matter," said Jane. "What are you doing?"

"I can't get her to sleep, so I thought I'd light the stove and try to give her some warm milk." Her voice sounded harassed and weary.

"Well, I'll light the stove," said Jane. "I know how. I did it this morning."

So while Mary went to pick up Chris, Jane lit the stone and put on the milk. Presently they were sitting in dressing gowns around the kitchen table. Jane had made cocoa for Mary and herself, and Chris had stopped crying for the time being. Mary suddenly smiled. "What a helpful girl you are," she said.

"I am not specially helpful," said Jane. "At home Mummy says I am often rather a trouble. But here it doesn't seem so difficult to help."

"I dare say it's because you can see how I need help. I do my best, but things get in such a muddle."

Jane found this a satisfactory statement. It was seldom, she found, that grownups were inclined to confess their own faults. Chris started to wail again. Her face was red, and Mary put a hand on her forehead. "Her head does seem rather hot," she said after a minute. "'The trouble is I always forget to feel it when she's well, so I'm never really sure how hot it ought to be."

"Mummy takes our temperatures," said Jane helpfully. "Have you a thermometer?"

Mary nodded and looked about vaguely. "I know it's somewhere," she said. "We so seldom get ill that I lose it between sicknesses."

"In the bathroom?" suggested Jane.

Mary's face brightened at once. "Of course!" she said. "Now I know. It's on the shelf with the blue bags in the laundry. I tried to take Priscilla's temperature one day. I thought she was sick, but she turned out not to be. How clever of you, Jane."

Jane got up and went to look. It was there, right enough, but actually beside the starch. As she returned, she said curiously, "Did Priscilla have a temperature?"

"I don't know," said Mary. "I find it's terribly hard to take a dog's temperature. And of course she wasn't sick after all, so no doubt it wouldn't register. Fortunately, babies are not so difficult." She took the thermometer and shook down the mercury. "I'll just pop it under her arm and then we'll see."

Christobel took kindly to being partially unpeeled, and they waited in comfortable silence for the minutes to pass. There is something about taking a temperature that is, in itself, consoling. After a glance at her watch, Mary removed the thermometer from Christobel's arm and held it up to the lamp. She frowned fearfully in her efforts to read it. Then she looked up at Jane, who sat watching her on the opposite side of the table.

"It's up a bit," she said. "It's about a hundred. I wonder if that means a serious illness or just a slight indisposition?" She gave a short, sharp sigh. "I wish the telephone were working."

"A hundred isn't much," said Jane. "I'm often a hundred when I have a cold. Daddy says it's my tonsils, but I never die of it, or anything."

"That's a mercy," said Mary, and added absently, "You'll have to have them out some day. I quite enjoyed having mine out—ice cream and presents in bed and not such a terribly sore throat." She looked down at Chris. "At any rate," she said, "now I know she's sick, so I must treat her like an invalid." She got up. "I'll put her to bed now, and perhaps she'll sleep." She looked closely at Jane. "And you must go to bed, too. I suppose I shouldn't have let you get up at all. You've had a very trying time. You'd better stay in bed late in the morning." At the door she suddenly paused. "I hope it's nothing catching," she said. "Your mother wouldn't like *that*." For a moment she peered into Jane's face, almost, Jane thought, as if she were already looking for germs on it. Then she gave a little sigh and carried Christobel off down the passage. Jane blew out the light and crept quietly to her own bed.

Next morning the storm had gone but left behind it a drizzle and low clouds.

"No flying today," said Vincent.

Jane showed no ill effects from her wakeful night, but at breakfast Mary looked tired and unusually depressed. They noticed that her face appeared smaller and more full of shadows, and her eyes had lost their brightness. Jane had told the boys about the happenings in the night, and they asked now whether Christobel was any better.

"I don't really think so," said Mary. "Her temperature hasn't gone down, and she's terribly grizzly."

As soon as they had done their morning jobs, Bobby and Vincent went to look for Skyraider. Jane remained in the house. There was plenty to do, for Mary now spent more time with Christobel. Once they turned the radio on and found that their story was now coming over the national stations. Except that the weather had prevented the air search, there was nothing new. Once more the thought of Mr. and Mrs. Thompson's anxiety upset Jane, and Mary said that until they were able to make a move in some direction or another, they would not listen again.

Toward lunchtime, when the house was clean and the cooking done and Christobel had at last fallen asleep, Mary, after a glance at Jane's tense face, said, "Shall we go quickly down to the river and back, just to see how high it is and what those boys are up to?"

"Oh, yes," said Jane, "I'd love to. But what about Chris?"

"Chris will sleep now for a while, and I think I'd like to go." Mary passed her hand in a puzzled way across her forehead. "I have a headache this morning, and I think some fresh air might take it away. We needn't be away long."

So they put on coats and Mary lent Jane a pair of gum boots, and they went down to the river. Priscilla bounded ponderously and sedately beside them. The air was fresh and reviving and smelled of growing things and damp earth. The valley was dank and sodden, and the surrounding hills were still shrouded in mist. They reached the water without seeing a sign of anyone or anything.

They had gone perhaps fifty yards upstream when Mary said, "Listen."

Somewhere ahead somebody was shouting. The sound came high and clear over the water. They hurried on, and very soon Jane recognized the craggy rocks and the steep, narrow river bed where the wire that Mary called the flying fox crossed the river. She looked to see if the wires were still there. Then she stopped dead and clutched Mary's arm. Words deserted her, but she pointed with her other hand.

"Good heavens!" said Mary. "He'll be killed." Then she rushed for dear life up the last few yards to the end of the flying fox.

The wires were there all right, and out in the middle of them, dangling on the pulley over the black chasm and the jagged rocks below, was Bobby. He was standing in a loop of rope that hung from the hook at the bottom of the pulley. With one hand he gripped the top of the pulley, and in the crook of his other arm, clutched against his side, was Skyraider. Skyraider's muzzle had that wrinkled look, as if he were about to whistle, that dogs get when they are frightened. They saw that his collar was around the hook that hung from the pulley. At the end of the wire, winding steadily and slowly, his eyes glued to that gently swinging bead on the wire necklace, was Vincent. Jane was about to rush up to him with an exclamation, but Mary held her firmly.

"Leave him alone," she said quickly. "We'll only do harm by interfering."

So they watched in silence as Bobby, with nerve-racking creaks and jerks, moved toward them. After what seemed to them hours, he reached the bank. Carefully, he unhooked Skyraider and put him down. Then he climbed off himself. Skyraider showed his relief by doing his best to jump up and down, but he was lame in one hind leg.

Then Jane and Mary descended upon them. "Bobby!" said Jane in furious tones. "You silly, stupid thing! What were you doing? You might have been killed. You know

it was broken." Both boys jumped guiltily. Before they had time to reply, Jane attacked again. "You might have strangled Skyraider," she said indignantly.

Bobby managed to say mildly, "Don't think so. Thought it'd be easier to stop him strangling than to catch him if he fell." Both boys were putting on their coats again.

"Well, now," said Mary, pouring oil on what threatened to be rather troubled waters, "we'll all go back for lunch.

I must hurry home to Chris, and you can tell us what happened as we go. How did you find Skyraider? And why is he lame?"

Vincent told them the story. They had gone downstream to look for Skyraider, knowing that he would have been washed some way before he could get out. They had had no trouble finding him, for they had only gone a little way past what they now called Priscilla's Crossing when they heard him howling. They followed the sound and were able to see on the far side of the river an old wire-netting fence that ran down to the water.

Mary nodded. "That would be our boundary," she said.

Poor Skyraider had tried to jump the fence, having presumably gotten out of the river some way down on the far side, and had been caught by the hind leg. Fortunately, he could reach the ground with his front ones, which probably saved his life. But he must have spent a very uncomfortable night. The question now was how to get over to extract him. They decided that the only thing to do was to go back to the machinery shed and fetch a length of fencing wire Bobby remembered seeing there and some tools in the hope that they could mend the flying fox.

They had hurried back, wheeled the pulley over to their side, and Bobby had gone across on it.

"But it was *broken!*" said Jane again.

"I know," said Vincent, "but we thought he'd better risk it. After all"—he paused for a minute—"he was the lightest, and he *could* have hung on to the top wire if it had broken."

"And Skyraider's my dog," said Bobby.

"Anyway," went on Vincent, "he got across all right and went down to let Skyraider go—"

"His toe's not broken, I don't think," said Bobby. "Only maybe a bit twisted. It's swelled up a bit."

"Then Bobby came back, and we managed to fix the new wire, and when we reckoned it was working properly, Bobby and Skyraider just—came back on it."

Suddenly and unexpectedly Mary laughed. "It all sounds so simple," she said.

Christobel was still asleep when they returned, but the walk seemed to have exhausted Mary. She ate very little lunch and afterward went off to have a sleep until Chris should wake again.

The boys helped Jane wash up. She told them about the morning's radio report.

"Well," said Bobby, "we can go now. We don't have to wait for the mailman."

"How can we go?" asked Jane.

"I suppose he means we can cross over on the wire," said Vincent slowly.

"On the flying fox?" said Jane in a high and horrified voice. "I couldn't."

"Oh, well," said Bobby. "Vince and I can go and tell them where you are. Can't we, Vince?"

It was hard to tell from Vincent's expression whether he agreed wholeheartedly with this idea or not. He contented himself with nodding.

"But you couldn't start this afternoon," said Jane. "It's too late now. Better wait till the morning. It might be sunny," she finished with a fine burst of optimism.

They agreed that it was better to wait. Neither of them felt like starting off again that day.

FOURTEEN
OUT OF THE VALLEY

They all went to bed early, but it was a bad night. Christobel was awake and crying for most of it, and once or twice they heard her screaming. Jane got up and did what she could to help. Mary confessed that she still had her headache, but eventually she sent Jane off unwillingly to bed, promising to go herself as soon as Chris seemed quieter.

In the morning the boys got up early, did all their jobs in good time, and prepared to leave. They did not see Mary until breakfast time. Jane said she had not seen her either and had managed to get the breakfast on her own. When Mary came in, she had no smile for them but sat down in her chair in the slow and rather stiff way that old people do. She would not have any breakfast, but asked Jane to pour her a cup of tea. She said nothing until it had been passed to her and she had taken some of it. Then she pushed the cup away and leaned back in her chair.

"I think I must tell you all," she said, "that I suspect

now that Chris may have polio. I don't know very much about its symptoms, but I remembered in the night that last time Jack and I went into town, we had dinner with some friends who had a sick child. At that time they thought it was only a cold, and he was still running about. He—he played with Chris. We had heard there had been cases of polio in the town, but of course we never thought of it. We heard, just as Jack was leaving, that the child is in hospital as a suspected case. I probably wouldn't have thought of it now if it wasn't that I have begun to feel rather peculiar myself, with a headache and a stiff neck and all that sort of thing." She stopped as if the effort of talking had tired her.

No one moved or said anything, and she went on, "Unfortunately the polio immunization scheme has been rather slow in coming to our town. It takes them such a long time to get all over the state, and of course they do the bigger centers first. Then I believe they ran out of serum for a time, and the children here have had only one of the injections." She closed her eyes for a moment and then continued, "It's not enough for safety. Ordinarily, I could ring Doctor Morton or take Chris straight in. But the river and the telephone. . . . I suppose it always might have happened before, but it never has." She stopped, shivered, and then said, "So I think that somehow or other I shall have to get Chris into town, and I shall have to do it before I feel any worse. If I'm going to be ill, too, I must see she's in the proper hands before— before it's too late." She looked at them each in turn, her eyes dark with tiredness and very wide, and they knew that she was frightened, but it was for Chris, not for herself.

Vincent, in the silence that followed, cleared his throat.

"Wouldn't it be better," he said, "if Bobby and I went in straight away? We'd be as quick as we possibly could, and we'd bring the doctor back to you. We can go now, you know—over the wire. You could wait quietly here. You'd have Jane."

But she was quite positive. "I must get in," she said again. "How could I wait here, wondering if you had found the way? Wondering if you had found the doctor? He's often miles away on cases. And then, how could he get here? Not even a Landrover could cross the river as it is now. I've thought it all out. I spent most of the night thinking it out, as a matter of fact. I've got to get across the river." She stopped again, then took a breath and said in a voice they had never heard her use before, "And I can't think how."

Bobby said, after a silence, "Don't you think you could risk the flying fox? I think it would hold you. You're not any heavier than Vincent. He could go first."

Nobody felt like smiling. Their eyes were on her face. Then she said, "But Chris and I—even if I could manage to carry her across, surely we'd be far too heavy?"

"One of us could carry her," said Jane.

"No!" said Mary immediately in such a voice that Jane wondered what she had done wrong. "The infection! I can't let you touch her. After all you've been through, imagine what I'd feel if you caught it! That's one of the things that's worrying me so. Unless—" She suddenly stopped and looked up quickly. "I never thought—perhaps you've all had your vaccines. Have you? That would relieve my mind enormously."

"No, I haven't," said Vincent quickly. "At least, not all of them. We're due to have the rest next term."

"And we—" began Jane, and then felt such a sudden,

sharp blow on her shin that she gave a little yelp of pain. She saw that Bobby was glaring at her and realized that the blow had been caused by his boot.

When he saw that his sister was effectively silenced, he said, "I can carry her across for you. I carried Skyraider across all right, and I'm the lightest."

"If you're sure you're safe from the infection—" Mary began, and Jane, silent with a smarting shin, saw Bobby's pale blue eyes gazing limpidly into Mary's face and his head giving the slightest of nods. "If you're quite sure, and—and—" She drew a deep breath. "I think we shall have to take the risk."

After that they wasted no more time. Mary went to prepare Chris for the long journey; Jane cleared away the breakfast things and, with a rare forethought that she seldom displayed at home, shut all the windows and filled the kerosene refrigerator. Bobby and Vincent went to look for straps and lengths of rope, and in a short time they were ready to leave. Chris was well and snugly wrapped up, but Mary wore only what she had on at breakfast. Jane said nothing but went away and returned a few minutes later with Mary's coat. She held it out, and Mary meekly slipped her arms in.

They stepped out of the door, Jane shut it behind them, and they started off toward the river. Priscilla and Skyraider followed in the rear.

When they reached the riverbank, Bobby turned to Vincent. "You'd better go first," he said, "and wind me over."

Silently, Vincent produced one of the pieces of rope, looped it around the hook, stepped into it as if it were a stirrup, reached up and grasped the top of the pulley, and announced that he was ready. Bobby wound him across.

Mary watched in silence and took a deep breath when he landed safely on the other side.

"Now," said Bobby when the pulley had returned. He held out his hands for Christobel.

"No!" said Mary, suddenly taking a step back. "No!"

Unaccountably, Bobby smiled, "It's all right," he said. "She'll be easier than Skyraider. I reckon we won't weigh any more than Vincent. I've got some straps." From his waist he unbuckled two belts. The third remained to support his trousers.

Mary slowly held out the baby. It seemed to cause her a great effort to do so. Bobby took hold of Christobel and balanced her carefully on his hip. There was not a very great deal of hip, but it was sufficient to take some of the weight. Then he handed Jane the belts and instructed her where to put them. One went under Christobel's arms and around his neck; the other strapped her waist firmly to his chest. One arm was around her, holding her securely; he went up to the pulley, put his foot in the loop and his own belt through the hook. He called over his shoulder to Jane, "Wheel me out till I'm just off the ground."

She did so, and he called out, "Whoa!" as his weight left the ground. With one toe just keeping himself steady, he proceeded to bounce and jerk on the rope. The wire ropes groaned and squeaked in protest, but they stood the test. When he was satisfied, he let himself off the rope and turned to Mary.

"Nothing wrong with that, is there?" he asked.

Mary seemed unable to reply, but she shook her head. Bobby once more put his weight on the pulley, took a firm grip, and called out to Vincent. Slowly he swung out into space, and little by little the pulley moved out across the river. Chris was quite still.

Jane, who had been watching, turned to Mary, who had sat down and had her hand over her eyes. Jane sat down beside her.

"It's all right," she said. "It's going beautifully."

She did not add that out there on the rope, away over the swiftly flowing river, Bobby looked very small indeed. Instead, she continued to watch and said nothing for a short time. Then she put her hand lightly on Mary's arm. Mary jumped as if she had been pricked.

"It's finished," Jane said. "They're there. They've arrived."

Mary opened her eyes and looked. Then she let out a long breath, and for the first time that day she smiled. But all she said was, "That Bobby."

The pulley returned, and from the other side Bobby called out that Jane was to go next. Alarmed but silent, she did as she was told. She clutched the pulley and shut her eyes. She felt herself swaying, screwed her eyes even tighter, and after what seemed a terribly long time felt a gentle bump at her feet. She gingerly opened her eyes, saw the ground beneath her, and with a huge sigh stepped off. Then Bobby took the pulley from her and swung himself onto it once more.

"Mind Chris," he said as he sailed out over the gorge.

He reached the bank, hopped off the pulley, and walked up to Mary. She looked down at him without moving. He was small, even for his age, and although she was not tall, his head only reached her chest. Unexpectedly, she put her hand on top of it. "It was a long way down, wasn't it?" she said.

"Quite safe," said Bobby a little more gruffly than usual. "Chris couldn't have fallen without me."

"I know," she said. "That's what I meant."

For a moment Bobby looked perplexed. Then he took her firmly by the hand. "Come on," he said. "Your turn."

She allowed herself to be led to the wire. When he asked her, a little anxiously, if she would prefer to sit in the loop, she shook her head. "I can manage," she said. "I shall do exactly what you tell me."

But he wouldn't let her go until he had strapped one of the belts around her waist and looped it over the hook. He showed her where to hold with her hands.

"Hang on," he ordered, and wheeled her out until her weight was on the rope. He stopped, returned to her, and made her bounce as he had done. When he saw that her efforts were too feeble, he hung on himself and bounced with her. When he was satisfied, he looked at her once more, perhaps with some anxiety, for she was looking very tired, and said finally, "Sure you feel O.K.?"

She nodded, and he signaled Vincent. He sat down, hugging his knees while she crossed. When she was half-way over the rope gave a little jerk, and he saw one of her hands lose its grip. He made a sudden move forward but saw the hand grab again at the pulley, catch it, and take a firm hold. He sat down again. She continued smoothly over the river. When she reached the other side and he saw Jane run down to help her, he sprang up, raced to the windlass, and drew the pulley back again. He stepped on, signaled once more to Vincent, and made his final trip across the river.

As they were leaving, the two dogs turned up, dripping wet.

"They've swum," said Vincent. "Skyraider probably thought it was safer."

After that they left the river and started on the long walk to the nearest house. The rain had gone, and it was a pleasant morning for walking—crisp and breezy, with moving tree shadows mottling the ground. They would have enjoyed it if it had not been for Christobel, who was making them uneasy by her quietness, and Mary, who would have to lead them and who already looked so tired. But she said nothing and kept steadily on, even if the pace was rather slow.

FIFTEEN
MRS. JONES IS SURPRISED

For a time they followed the track that had led them in, but before long Mary turned off it and followed a track so faint that they would never have found it on their own. It was shorter, she said, than following the car track. It took them leftward down the hill, across a little creek, and up a long hill on the other side. And it was here that they first began to wonder whether Mary would be able to reach the end. As she climbed the hill, her breathing turned into short, painful gasps, her steps became slower and very short, and twice before they reached the top of the hill she had to stop and rest.

It was during one of these rests, when they happened to be sitting under a wattle tree in a piece of particularly thick scrub, that Vincent suddenly held up his hand and cocked his head sideways. He remained motionless for a second and then said, "Hear it?"

"No," said Jane, taking a piece of grass out of her mouth. "What?"

"Listen," he said.

They all listened. And above the rustle of leaves, the soughing of branches, and the chirp of birds, they heard a faint hum.

"Sounds like bees," said Jane. "Perhaps it's a swarm."

"Silly," said Bobby. "It's an airplane."

"Yes, and it's getting louder," said Vincent.

Even then the significance did not dawn on them at once. The noise gradually increased.

"Low, isn't it?" said Jane. Then she suddenly remembered and sprang to her feet. "Why," she screeched, "it's looking for us!"

They all jumped up, except Mary, who sat with her eyes half closed, and they wondered if she heard it at all. The noise grew louder and louder, became a roar that filled the sky and seemed to rattle the leaves, and they saw a small Auster aircraft skimming the treetops just above them. They even caught a glimpse of the pilot's head, peering down through his windshield. They shouted, waved, and ran about, throwing their hats and coats into the air. It seemed impossible that he shouldn't have seen them. But the sound faded again, dropped from a roar to a drone, became a thin little sound in the distance, and finally disappeared entirely.

"Oh!" said Jane, and sat down again with a bump. "He must be blind."

But Vincent shook his head. "He'd never see us through these trees. If only we'd had a fire going." He stopped and put his hand in his pocket. "Shall we light one? I've got some matches."

"No," said Bobby shortly, picking up Chris. "Probably

he won't come back, and we've got to keep going." He looked at Mary, who had opened her eyes and was beginning to move. "You help her up," he said to Jane. "And push her up the hill."

In this way, very slowly, they managed to reach the top. They found themselves on a ridge that ran for some distance toward the south and then fell away in a series of low green hills that had been cleared and sown with clover. Sheep grazed on them. And farther still, at the head of a wide green valley, they could see a homestead. Beyond the valley the country stretched out cleared and rolling. A road wound down the valley and out into the open country. In the far distance a huddle of little houses, sunk in clumps of trees far greener than the wild eucalypti, told them that they had reached civilization once more.

But not quite. There was still a fair walk to the homestead, and Mary's progress was becoming constantly slower. Once Vincent asked if he should go on ahead and bring back help, for the track was now more clearly marked and there would not be many places from which he could not see the house. But she shook her head, and they kept on. Jane and Mary were now walking with linked arms, and it was clear that Mary was glad of that sturdy support. Once Vincent offered his arm also, but when Mary quickly told him to keep away from her, he did not insist. Jane looked at him with a little puzzled frown.

Eventually, some time after midday, according to Vincent's calculations, they descended the last gentle slope and saw the homestead lying in front of them only a little distance away. Like their own house, it was a compact, square brick building, made to look slightly larger than it was by the veranda that ran around three sides of it. The corrugated iron roof of the house and the curved iron roof of the veranda were painted with red oxide, now somewhat faded. A small rectangular garden in front was bounded by a neat privet hedge. The usual collection of sheds, yards, dog kennels, and farm machinery clustered around the back of the house. Smoke was coming out of the chimney.

"Look," said Bobby over the top of Christobel's head. "Telephone lines."

And now Vincent, who was leading, turned and said, "I'm going to run on ahead and warn them we're coming. They can start to get beds ready." This time Mary said nothing. Jane wondered if she even knew where she was. For the last mile she had almost seemed to be asleep. Vincent raced across the paddock, and they saw him disappear around the corner of the hedge and make for the back yard. He was sufficiently used to the country to know that the life of a farmhouse is always at the back and never along that rather forbidding front veranda.

There was no gate at the back, but the track led him straight to the garage beside the back door. He noticed, without giving the fact much thought, that it was empty. He was just about to climb the steps to the back door when he heard a gate click. He turned and waited. A girl of about twelve appeared around the corner of one of the sheds, carrying an empty tomato-sauce bottle with a baby's nipple on the end of it.

"Excuse me," said Vincent in rather a lordly way. "Are your father or mother about anywhere?"

She approached him in silence, and he noticed that her face and neck were brown and her fair hair was bleached almost white by the sun. She wore a pair of jeans and a cotton shirt.

She looked at him with wide eyes and an expressionless face. And then, apparently having absorbed all she wished, she said, "I don't know. I been feeding the lamb. Dad's away, but Mum's about somewhere." She continued on to the house, and Vincent, a little nonplussed, followed. When she reached the back veranda, she put one foot on the step and called, "You there, Mum?" A faint cry from the interior answered her and she called again, "A chap here wants you."

She gave Vincent a nod, said, "She'll be out in a jiff," and went off around the side of the house. Vincent, considering the weight of the news he bore, felt that his welcome was scarcely appropriate. But then the back door opened and a short, round, businesslike woman confronted him. She gave him a friendly smile.

"Didn't hear you come," she said. "Where's your car?"

When Vincent explained he had come on foot, she gave a little exclamation of astonishment. He went on quickly, "We've brought Mary Taylor and Christobel. She says you know her. They're both very sick, and the phone's out of order. We have had quite a time getting them across the river." He paused and then said, "I'm sorry to have to tell you they probably have polio, so they're infectious."

"Oh, my goodness," said the lady. "What a terrible thing! And where are they? I shall have to get them to bed at once and ring the doctor." She looked about as if she might have overlooked them standing about in the yard.

"My cousins are bringing them," said Vincent. "I couldn't help much because I haven't been properly immunized." He said it in an apologetic tone, but the lady nodded. "Of course not. You have to be careful. Now you tell me where they are and I'll go and help bring them in. That poor Mary. Such a nice girl, too." She shook her head and tut-tutted in a very sympathetic way. Then she turned and called loudly, "Amy! You there, Amy?"

"Yes," answered the girl's voice from a distance.

"You come and ring the doctor quick. Tell him to come here quick as he can. Might be polio, tell him. And then you make up the spare-room bed and get down the cot. Hurry now!" She paused only to draw breath and then said to Vincent, "Come on. Show me where they are. My gracious, what a thing to happen when Jack's away! That poor girl, and the little baby, too." She talked as she walked, but it did not impede her progress, and Vincent had trouble to keep up. As soon as she saw the little group coming so slowly up the track, she broke into a run.

Mary was now leaning heavily on Jane, who was showing a tendency to buckle at the knees, and Bobby, with Chris still in his arms, was on the point of exhaustion. The lady, her apron billowing, for she had omitted to take it off, approached them at speed, snatched Chris from Bobby's arms, grasped Mary firmly around the waist with her other hand, and said in tones of great distress, "My poor girl, whatever has been happening to you. If we'd only known, we'd have come over quick and lively in the old truck. Well, thank goodness you're here. We'll soon have you in bed." She glanced around at the drooping figures beside her. "And you little children, too"—she did not notice Bobby's dreadful frown —"I'll get you fixed up in a jiffy. What a good thing you had this big boy to help you." She continued talking until they reached the house. Then she called once more for Amy, told the children to wait in the kitchen, and disappeared down the passage with her two invalids. The children sat and looked at one another. They did not doubt that what the lady said was true. They did feel lucky to have Vincent. He could speak to strangers without any trouble at all, and the way he had everything organized so quickly here showed how necessary he was to them. Before anyone had mustered sufficient energy to say anything, there was a slight movement at the door. They looked around to see a boy standing there observing them in silence. Vincent saw that he was a slightly smaller counterpart of Amy, bleached, browned, and silent.

"Hullo," said Vincent. "I suppose you're Amy's brother?"

The boy apparently thought this scarcely worth answering, for he said simply, "What's up?"

"We've just brought in a sick person," said Vincent, and was prepared to elaborate further, but the boy interrupted him.

"I know. Heard Amy telephoning the doctor. Who is it? What's he done?"

They told him, and they thought he was impressed, though his face showed nothing. He turned his attention to Bobby, and for a few minutes they eyed each other, suspicion and dislike now plain in each face. Then the boy said, "My name's Trevor. What's yours?"

"His name's Bobby," said Jane brightly before Bobby could answer.

"Bobby!" Trevor repeated it, and there was a curl to

his lip as he said it. Bobby said nothing, but his eyebrows twitched.

At that moment the lady bustled back into the kitchen. It was quite some time before they discovered that her name was Mrs. Jones. She went to the stove, filled the kettle, and put it on.

"They're sick, all right," she said. "It was lucky you got them here when you did. I hope the doctor comes soon." She swung around and said, "Do you like milk or tea? There's both."

They decided on tea, and she clapped some cups and saucers on the table. "It's just bad luck," she went on. "Dad's out with the car helping the police look for those kids. Otherwise, we could take them straight to town. Can't be helped." A big fruit cake arrived on the table, and she cut it with great, sweeping strokes. "There you are. Help yourselves." She stopped, noticing that three pairs of wide-open eyes were gazing at her. "Well," she said, "what's the matter?"

"We forgot," said Vincent. "We forgot to tell you. We're them."

Mrs. Jones looked understandably puzzled. "I beg yours?" she said politely.

"We're the kids. The ones Mr. Jones is looking for," explained Jane. "Perhaps you ought to ring up about us, too. We think Mummy is worrying."

Dead silence greeted this piece of information. Mrs. Jones put down the knife and kettle the better to concentrate her gaze; Amy and Trevor approached silently from different corners of the room.

"You mean," said Mrs. Jones at last in a high, loud voice. "You mean you're those Thompson children they've all been looking for all this time?" She sat down suddenly and passed her hand over her face.

"Yes," said Jane. "And we knew they were looking for us, but you see we couldn't cross the river and the phone was out of order, so we couldn't tell them. But perhaps we ought to now." Her voice was diffident and apologetic. But Mrs. Jones sprang up with dramatic suddenness.

"Amy! Trevor!" she shouted in clarion tones. "See these children have all they want to eat. Give them plenty of tea. Maybe they need some clothes. I'd better get on to that telephone." She disappeared through the door, and they heard her attacking the telephone with violence.

Amy and Trevor silently approached the table. Vincent, Jane, and Bobby said nothing. They could afford to. After a time Trevor said, "They been looking for you with airplanes."

Bobby raised one eyebrow and looked at him. "Why not?" he said. He had not forgotten the curled lip.

"Here," said Amy suddenly and, reaching over, gave the cake a shove that nearly propelled it off the table. "Better have some more cake."

"Want another cupper tea?" said Trevor, staggering from the stove with the teapot.

They allowed their cups to be refilled. They took frequent small pieces of cake. The occasion was not without its pleasant side.

Before long Mrs. Jones returned with the complacent look of one who had been the bearer of weighty and joyful news.

"The doctor's on his way," she said. "And they're sending the ambulance and the policeman, and you're to go back with them in the ambulance." She sat down and slapped the palms of her hands on the table. "Well, I've never been more dumfounded in all me life," she announced with satisfaction.

After that it did not seem long until the arrival of the doctor. Mrs. Jones spent it in a frustrated whirl, partly in the sick room and partly sitting enthralled on the kitchen chair while they told her their adventures. Amy and Trevor draped themselves over the back of her chair and never moved their eyes. From time to time their mouths fell open. Vincent and Jane shared the recital, while Bobby listened with an interest as absorbed as the Jones's. There were bits that surprised him, too.

When the doctor came, Mrs. Jones bustled him into the bedroom. Before he came out again, the ambulance had arrived, and the kitchen suddenly became full of large people all talking at once. A grim-faced policeman bore down on the children, and they were disposed to shrink back and utter monosyllabic replies until they noticed the Jones children following him around and chewing sweets that he was producing from his pockets. Then they relaxed and told their story once again, as they were to tell it many times more before they finally reached home.

Presently the doctor returned to the kitchen and dropped his bag on the table.

"You can take them now," he said to the ambulance men. "Mrs. Jones will give you a hand to get them ready." He went over to the sink and washed his hands.

"Is it—I mean, have they got polio?" asked Vincent in a strained voice.

The doctor's gaze traveled from one anxious face to another. When he spoke, he chose his words carefully. "They're both quite sick. Of course you realize that, but

at this stage I wouldn't like to guess what it might be. It could be quite a number of less serious things. But we'll take no chances, and the sooner they get to hospital, the better. It's a great pity we had that delay with the injections." He looked at them curiously. "You're the three lost kids, are you?"

"Yes," said Vincent with a touch of pride.

"How do you feel? All right?"

They assured him that they never felt better, and after that the ambulance men came in with the stretchers and they all made a move outside. The policeman said, "We'll send the three kids back in the front of the ambulance. You going straight away, doc?" The doctor nodded. "I'll come with you if you don't mind. I'll have to get going and call off this search."

Trevor had disappeared for a few minutes, but now he returned and sidled up to Bobby. He slipped something into Bobby's hand.

"Better have this," he mumbled. "I got dozens."

Bobby opened his hand and looked at the contents. It was a sheath knife a good deal superior to his own broken-bladed one at home, and it had a proper leather sheath. But he turned it over in his hand several times, drew it out of the sheath, and ran his finger along the blade; it was razor-sharp and ideal for skinning rabbits. Trevor watched him with silent absorption. Finally Bobby looked up.

"Not a bad knife," he said casually. "Thanks, Trev." He slipped it into his pocket, and Trevor allowed a brief but satisfied smile to cross his face.

A hitch occurred as they were getting into the ambulance. Bobby was already in, and Vincent, the last to come, was about to step in when Bobby began to struggle out again.

"Hey, what's up?" said the driver. "We got to go."

Bobby said nothing but continued to scramble painfully over Jane. He ignored her complaints also. Once out of the vehicle, he put his fingers to his mouth and produced an earsplitting whistle. He did it twice and the second time was rewarded by the whirlwind appearance of Priscilla and Skyraider. He waved his hand, and they jumped up into the ambulance.

"Hey!" said the driver again, this time with great indignation. "We don't carry dogs in the ambulance."

Bobby stood back and whistled again. The dogs jumped out. "I'll stay," he announced. "Tell Mum I'll be along pretty soon."

"Now, dear," said Mrs. Jones, bearing down on him, "you go along. I'll look after your dogs. They'll be quite safe." Bobby side-stepped as she appeared about to pick him up bodily. He shook his head. "I'd rather stay, thanks."

"Oh, cripes," said the driver, "we've got to go. We've got sick people behind. All right, let 'em all come. Cost me my job, probably."

So the three children and the two dogs somehow fitted in beside the driver, and the ambulance moved off. Mrs. Jones, Amy, and Trevor stood side by side and mournfully waved good-by. Their hour of glory was over.

SIXTEEN
RELUCTANT HERO

It took them three quarters of an hour to reach the township, for the road was bad and the driver did not want to shake the patients more than necessary. After Mary and Chris were delivered to the hospital, the children were taken to the police station. They had wanted to say good-by to Mary but were told that she was sleeping and they might be able to see her in the morning.

At the police station there was a message saying that Mr. and Mrs. Thompson would be arriving in the evening and they were to wait there until called for. It was now getting on to six, and very soon groups of men started to arrive in cars, trucks, and Landrovers. They all came into the police station looking tired, dusty, and tattered. These were the men, the policeman told them, who had spent the day looking for them in the hills. It was Vincent who went and spoke to them and thanked them all very nicely for what they had done.

For the first time in their lives Jane and Bobby found themselves the center of a great deal of attention. They told their story over and over again; a reporter and a photographer from a country newspaper, who blessed their good fortune in having chosen this town from which to try to gather news, came and asked them questions and took their photographs; people who had heard the news came and gathered curiously at the gate and waited patiently to catch a glimpse of them. Vincent enjoyed it, Jane took it in her stride, and only Bobby looked as if he were undergoing a mild form of torture. Even the dogs, when their part of the story came and they were patted and admired, entered into the spirit of rejoicing.

They were sitting in the kitchen in the policeman's house, and the policeman's wife had just given them supper when Mr. and Mrs. Thompson arrived. They both looked very tired, and the children were surprised to find how old their parents had become. Jane flung herself into her mother's arms with a squeak of joy, and Mr. Thompson put an arm around each of the boys.

"Well, well," he said. And then he said it again. When he had said it a third time, Mrs. Thompson disentangled herself from Jane, pushed her to arms' length, and looked her up and down.

"You naughty, naughty children," she said fondly. "What can you have been thinking of to cause us so much trouble?"

So they recited their story once more, and this time they had the best audience of all, for Mrs. Thompson kept exclaiming and Mr. Thompson kept making them repeat bits that he was not quite clear about. As they told it, Mrs. Thompson sat on a chair and absently pulled at Skyraider's ears. Even when he jumped onto her lap and curled himself, dirty and smelly as he was, on her clean skirt, she did not appear to notice and went on pulling his ears. When it was over, Mr. Thompson thanked the policeman and said that they would all stay in town that night because he wanted to try to see Mary in the morning.

They went off into the cool autumn night, and now the wind had dropped and all the stars were sparkling. The two dogs went with them, and because by this time they were quite famous, the hotel did not complain when Mr. Thompson said that they would be bringing the dogs as well.

Jane was almost asleep in the bed beside her mother when she suddenly sat up and exclaimed, "Our ponies! Mum, how are our ponies?"

"Too fat," said her mother comfortably. "Far, far too fat. Father brought them home, and now you'll have to ride them hard or they'll be foundering. They had heaps to eat in the paddock where you left them."

"Goody," said Jane, sighed deeply, and fell asleep.

The next day they found that they were not allowed to see Mary until after lunch. They were told that her husband had returned and was with her. The hospital told them guardedly that she had had a good night and was better. They might see her at two o'clock.

"That must mean that she's not infectious," said Mr. Thompson.

At two o'clock they presented themselves, were allowed in, and were met at her door by a tall young man with untidy hair and a cheerful face. "Mary's been waiting for you," he said at once. "Please come in."

"Is she—can we—" began Mrs. Thompson, and he replied quickly, "It's all right. The doctor told us definitely this morning it isn't polio. One of those new viruses with somewhat similar symptoms." He laughed suddenly. "I can tell you I was glad to hear it." He held the door open. "The doctor says the infectious period is over now. You'll be quite safe!"

They went in. Mary was lying contentedly in bed, and if she did not look exactly robust, her welcoming smile was very cheerful. Her eyes flicked over them all, found what they were looking for, and she held out her hand.

"That Bobby," she said for the second time.

Bobby gave her a sheepish smile and took her hand. Jack, and then Mr. and Mrs. Thompson were introduced, and Jack said, "I've just been hearing how much these three did for Mary and Chris, and I can't tell you how grateful I am. What she'd have done if they hadn't been there, I can't think."

Mary spoke from the bed. "I'm sure they wouldn't have told you everything, Mrs. Thompson. You tell them, Jack." And once again the Thompsons listened to the story. But this time there was a difference, and they looked as if they were enjoying it even more.

When Jack came to the part where they had all decided that Bobby had better carry Chris because Vincent was not immune to the infection, Mrs. Thompson gave a little cry. "But Bobby and Jane have never been immunized either," she said. "When we were out west, it always meant such a long drive into town. We were one hundred miles out, you see, and with the three injections, it would have meant such a lot of traveling. So, knowing we were soon moving in, we rather left it. They were to be done next term when the new series of injections starts. It just shows," she ended emphatically, "that when it's a question of health, one should *never* feel anything is too much trouble."

There was a pause. Then Mary said quietly from the bed, "Did you know that, Bobby?"

Bobby's face became a rich scarlet, and he nodded.

"I meant to tell, but Bobby kicked me," said Jane.

"Oh, dearies," said Mrs. Thompson, and put her hand to her mouth.

"Now don't get steam up, Frances," said Mr. Thompson. "It wasn't polio." He spoke casually, but his eyes rested warmly on his squirming son.

After that quite a number of awkward and embarrassing things happened. For a time Jane felt that her world was tottering when Vincent said loudly, "Then Bobby's a jolly sight braver than I am. He knew as well as I did what a risk he was running—even more than me, because I'd had at least one injection. In fact, come to think of it, he's been running the whole show, really." He leaned over and gave Bobby a series of resounding thumps on the back. Bobby staggered, looking dazed and embarrassed, but gratified.

Then, somehow, word got around the town, and several reporters, who had failed to reach the little township till now, got hold of the story, and Bobby found that he had become an unwilling hero. Jane and Vincent, too, came in for their share of renewed publicity, and before Mr. and Mrs. Thompson were able to get them safely home, Bobby had the unhappy experience of seeing his photograph in several newspapers and his name in headlines. They suspected that Jack had spread the story, but he never admitted it, although he did confess that he had answered one or two questions that were put to him.

When the schoolmaster suggested that Bobby might meet the children of the town and when the Country Women's Association ladies had threatened to give a party, Bobby begged to be taken home. They went to say a last good-by to Mary. Chris was now much improved and was sitting on Mary's bed. Mary asked them if they would stay with her again when she was better, and they agreed enthusiastically.

Then Jack said to Bobby, "Anything you've been wanting specially lately? A watch, new horse, model airplane? Something like that?"

Bobby thought for a moment, looked up at him, and said in a voice so hoarse that it was almost no voice at all, "Call me Robert."

"I beg your pardon?" said Jack.

"Call me Robert," said Bobby once more, and his voice grated in his throat like the first crow of a cockerel.

"I'm sorry," said Jack, bending down. "Just say it once more."

"He says," translated Jane loudly, " 'Call me Robert.' "

"Oh," said Jack. "Yes, of course we will. Now, Robert, what would you like?"

Once more and very loudly, Bobby croaked, "Call me Robert." His face bore a harassed frown. "I mean," he added, "call me Robert."

Jack, now quite puzzled, bent down once more. But Jane came to the rescue again. "He means," she explained, "that the thing he wants is for you to call him Robert."

There was a silence. Bobby's face relaxed.

"I see," said Jack at last, and straightened himself. If

anyone expected to see him smile, they were disappointed. "We shall do that, of course. I think we ought to have thought of it for ourselves. Perhaps, then, we might leave the rest for the present. I have a feeling the Taylors and the Thompsons will be seeing a good deal of one another in the future." And as he said it, he did not look displeased with the prospect.

As Mr. and Mrs. Thompson, Vincent, Jane, and Bobby walked down the polished linoleum corridor of the hospital, Bobby brought up the rear, and contrary to hospital regulations, he was whistling through his teeth.